T0077971

Journey
Into
Yesterday

SIDNEY OWITZ

authorHOUSE

AuthorHouse™
1663 Liberty Drive
Bloomington, IN 47403
www.authorhouse.com
Phone: 833-262-8899

This is a work of fiction. All of the characters, names, incidents, organizations, and dialogue in this novel are either the products of the author's imagination or are used fictitiously.

Published by AuthorHouse 04/26/2022

ISBN: 978-1-6655-5821-1 (sc)
ISBN: 978-1-6655-5820-4 (e)

Print information available on the last page.

This book is printed on acid-free paper.

DEDICATION

This book is dedicated to the memory of my late mother and father, Yette and Sam.

CONTENTS

THE MAN I NEVER KNEW

*H*e was a quiet man, an honest man and a gentle person. He was hard-working, spoke little, and his only goal in life was to be able to take care of his family. He wanted no riches, and required very little for himself. He never took a vacation. He had minimal education; his only schooling was elementary and occurred while he was still in Lithuania, the land of his birth. He left Lithuania at the age of eleven, with his sister who was two years older, for another country – South Africa. At that time Lithuania was under Russian rule. Life in a Russian satellite country was rigorous for a Jew. There was anti-Semitism and there were pogroms, and young Jewish teen-agers were swept up as fodder for the Russian military machine. Young Jewish men did not wish to give their lives for a despotic czar who had been persecuting them. Their parents advised them to leave their country and to go and have a better life elsewhere.

His elder brother, Philip, had already left Lithuania for South Africa a few years prior to his departure in order to escape the Russian army, and had written home that South Africa was a marvelous land where the sun always shone and where one could easily make a living and live in peace, and never be called up to fight in any army as the country was protected by Great Britain. Pack up and come to this heavenly country, a land of freedom. The parents said "We are too old to start a new life in another country. We can't even afford to leave. But our two other children, let them go. They deserve a good life. We hope we will see them again someday."

So, Sam and his elder sister, Sarah, went off alone across the world to South Africa, without being able to speak any language other than

1

Yiddish. They crossed Europe in trains, and the English Channel by ship, and finally embarked from Southampton to sail to Cape Town. They undertook this Herculean task, without being able to converse with any people on land or any passengers at sea. In Cape Town they boarded a train to Johannesburg, one thousand miles away, where they had arranged to meet their big brother, Philip, at the railway station.

Big Brother Philip was not there. They waited a few hours like waifs in a foreign land with silent mouths, unable to speak or understand anybody and unable to ask questions, and Philip still did not come. They went outside the station, and saw a horse and cart waiting to pick up people. This was the taxi service at the turn of the century. Remember, there were no cars in those days – I am talking of 1899 or 1900. They showed the cart driver an address on a piece of paper which had been given to them by their parents before departure – the address of friends from Lithuania who had gone to South Africa. The driver of the cart nodded. He understood what they had wanted. They took their luggage, jumped on the cart, and went jogging down the Johannesburg streets until they came to a mine dump and shaft – except there were no houses in the vicinity, only a few stores. The driver stopped the cart, helped them off with their luggage and awaited payment. He seemed to understand that they would go into the store and get money from the store-keeper.

They edged their way in to the store, walking in between customers, not knowing if they were at the right address as they had expected to be delivered to a home. The customers were all black people. It all looked so foreign to them. They finally saw a white man. He must be the owner. They walked up to him, not remembering who he was and he not recognizing who they were, either. They looked at each other in an uncomfortable silence until the big sister announced in Yiddish who they were. "Yes" he said "I know your parents very well. When I last saw you, you were toddlers. What can you be doing here?!" He went out and paid for their horse-cab.

They told him – his name was Mr. Rubenstein - that their brother Philip was not at the railway station to meet them. He said there must have been some mistake. He had seen Philip on a few occasions, and would be able to find him for them on the following day.

"In the mean-time you will stay with me. I have a small house, so

Sarah, you will come home with me after I close the store, and you, Sam, will have to sleep in the store tonight because I have no bed or space for you. But first we will walk to my house and eat. Then I will walk you back to my store."

They had dinner at his house, prepared by his wife. The Rubensteins asked many questions about the people of their old home-town. Then Mr. Rubenstein and Sam walked back to the store so Sam could spend the night there. It had already turned dark when Mr. Rubenstein locked him in the store and told him that he would be back early the next morning.

It was a rather scary situation for Sam. After a prolonged trip and looking forward to meeting his big brother whom he had not seen for many years, there was no brother there. Now he was locked in to a store in a foreign country, surrounded by strange people that he had never come across before. He had heard stories of these strange people in Africa and how uncivilized they were. He felt very lonely and unrelaxed, but he tried to find a comfortable spot on the floor so he could get some sleep. He was very tired after such a long and unforgettable day, and tried to fall asleep, but sleep would not come. Then he heard some scratching noises and sounds of little creatures scampering along the floor next to him. There must be rats here! No, he could not sleep on the floor. He decided to sleep on top of the counter, where the rats certainly would not dare to be present. It did not take long for him to change his mind, as there were sounds of scratching and scampering right on the counter next to him. He did not wish to walk around in this zoo-like environment, nor did he wish to be confined to the counter-top. He spent the rest of the night in fear and waiting for his deliverer to unlock the door and come back into the store.

At last, he heard the tampering on the door bolt, and in came his savior, Mr. Rubenstein, who brought him some breakfast. It was not on that day, nor the next, but the following week-end that he and Sarah were taken on another horse-cab ride with Mr. Rubenstein, when they finally saw Philip. He was less friendly than they had anticipated – a little cold and aloof. There was no joy in his eyes when seeing his siblings after so many years in a strange land. He said he did not come to the station because he was too busy in the furniture store where he worked – in fact, he was rather busy even now - and promised to see them again soon. He had one bit of advice for his siblings. "There are no free lunches. If you need something, you have got to work for it." They did not expect such harsh instructions from a supposedly sympathetic brother. "Look at me" said Big Brother, "I am making a good living because I work hard. Soon I am going to open my own furniture store."

They went away with Mr. Rubenstein feeling disappointed as the only thread to living in this new land had been Philip – and he seemed to be proud of his own achievements and unwilling to give them a hand or an optimistic suggestion. They felt alone and lost in the jungles of Africa. The only light in the dark tunnel had been that Philip was there for them, but now the light seemed very dim.

Thanks to the Rubensteins who were becoming their only hope. They continued to live with them. They managed to find space for Sam in the house when he described his experience with the rats. Sarah was enrolled in a school, and Sam stayed with Saul Rubenstein and worked in the store. He tidied up the display of articles and moved clothing and other goods around to different places for him, and also kept his eyes open for possible theft, which took place constantly. If he noticed anything suspicious, he would tell Saul who would immediately investigate. The only schooling Sam received was that a Hebrew teacher came to the house a few times per week to give him Barmitzvah lessons as he would be turning 13 in a few months.

In fact, on the day he turned 13 Saul and Bessie (his wife) and Sarah came with him to the local synagogue where Sam recited a Portion of the Law and the prayers for his Barmitzvah. They also invited a few people for a small party at their house. This was during the time when the Anglo-Boer War was being fought out in South Africa – 1899 to 1902. The Afrikaners were fighting a guerilla war against the British Empire, holding them at bay for three years.

However, Sam continued to work for Saul Rubenstein for a small salary until Saul suggested that he go and work for his friend who had a similar store on the mine. Saul told Sam that his friend would give him a better salary as he really needed a hand - and Sam was now experienced in the trade!

They went to visit Philip infrequently as the years passed by as Philip showed no signs of becoming more friendly or helpful. He was rather critical, egging Sam on to get his own business and become his own boss as he had done. Philip had his own furniture store, and apparently was making a fine living. At this stage Sam was in his twenties. As a matter of fact, he had come a long way in his work. He was learning to speak English, and using the language as often as he could. He could converse in Bantu languages with his customers, recognizing the nuances of the different dialects.

You must understand that the Bantu were coming from all over Central Africa to work on the Witwatersrand gold mines, the largest in the world. They all spoke different Bantu languages. As a matter of fact, in order to prevent the problems of the Tower of Babel, they developed a universal language where all Bantu miners could understand each other, by borrowing words and phrases from all their languages so as to maintain conversation with each other. It was called "fanakalo", which means "like this", as when a boss on the mine was describing to a miner what he wanted done, he would show them and say "like this".

Sam rented space at a different shaft on the gold mine so as not to compete with his former bosses, and opened his own store. It thrilled him to see that this store was created by his own hands, and that he was doing very well on his own, even though his brother refused to lend him any money to help him start the business. Sam was doing all his own buying and selling. He had nobody to help him. He worked every day of the week, knew few people, and did not know what relaxation meant. To him, life was work.

He felt it was time to get married and have his own family. Philip was married and had two children and Sarah had already married, too. With the help of a match-maker he met a few women, none of whom excited him. Finally, he was introduced to Yette, and that was something else! They both liked each other at first sight.

They soon decided to marry, and Yette invited Sam to her home to meet her parents. At a later date, the rest of her family, too, were invited. Yette's father, Moishe, was problem number one. He was a wealthy man in the dairy business. He also owned a lot of property. He came from a religious family, where there had been much learning and a fair amount of wealth. One of his sons – Yette's brother - was a rabbi with major qualifications and the Chief Rabbi of the Beth Din (ecclesiastical court) in Johannesburg. Moishe said to Yette "You can't marry him. He has no money. You and your children will starve. He has no education. He has no 'yichas' (good family history). Forget about him. We will find someone else." Yette was adamant. No, I want Sam.

Moishe's family and Sam seemed to come from two different worlds. Moishe and his family were interested in money and gaining wealth. They were religious, spending much time in prayer and at the synagogue. Sam was struggling to make a living, knew few people and displayed no religious qualities.

Despite a lack of enthusiasm from all other members of her family, Yette married Sam. Lest you have not guessed this thus far, Sam and Yette were my parents. They bought a small house in a quiet suburb on the outskirts of Johannesburg, called Booysens Reserve. They had three children. Harry was the first. He was not born in a hospital with an obstetrician in attendance, as money was scarce. Consequently, Yette had a prolonged labor, difficult delivery, and Harry was born with cerebral palsy. After that unfortunate delivery, Yette had my sister, Lily, in a hospital, as they feared a possible repetition of the first delivery. I was the third child, also born in a hospital. Shortly after my birth Sam went bankrupt, his business having failed. He turned to his brother, Philip, for help, but none was forthcoming. He then asked Moishe, Yette's father - and Yette also asked her father - for a loan.

Moishe said to Yette "I warned you about this no-good man. I told you not to marry him. I said that you and your children would starve if you married him. I will not give him a penny. If I did, he would lose that, too. You and your children can come and live with me, but he can search for another place to live. I will not take him into my house! He will never set foot in my home again and you will never see him again!"

In those days divorce was a disgrace. Nobody should hear that Moishe's daughter was divorced! They would just have to live apart and never see each other again, and Yette would remain a single parent. We lived in our grandfather's house at his expense. His wife had already passed away. My mother did the cooking, the house-work and took care of the three children. We went off to school every day.

I was brought up believing that I did not have a father. I could not remember my father. I was never told what had happened to him. His name was never mentioned in the house. If my siblings would attempt to talk about him my mother would hush them up quickly before my grandfather could hear them. My mother would never refer to my father as she did not want to upset her father. My siblings soon learned that they dare not discuss my father in front of grandpa. His name and very existence was extinguished from our lives. Growing up I was sure that I was fatherless.

All the other kids I knew had fathers. I remember being teased "You don't have a father". I could not argue with them because I knew that they were right. I had no father. Once, my sister mentioned his name as someone of the past, but my grandfather told her never to mention his name again, as though he did not exist. Nor did other members of the family ever talk of my father. He had come and gone!

One day my mother said to me "Put on your best clothes. We are going out."

"Where are we going?" I asked.

"We are going to the park?' she answered.

"I never wear my best clothes when I go to the park" I retorted.

"Don't argue. Just get dressed nicely".

I got dressed in my best clothes and we went to the park. When we arrived there, I saw a man waiting to greet us. He grabbed hold of me and smothered me with kisses. We sat down on a bench, and he placed me on his lap, kissing me and giving me chocolates and candy. He put coins in my hand and he showed me tricks. When we walked he held my hand. Finally, we said good-bye and he had tears in his eyes. Then we went home.

On the way home my mother made me promise that I would not tell my brother and sister that we met a man. Nor was I to tell my grandfather that we met him. I kept my word. My mother thought that if I told my siblings, who were older and wiser than I was, they would mention it to my grandfather. My brother and sister were older than me ; hence, they were wiser and might talk. Of course, the man that we met was my father, but I did not know it then. When I asked my mother who he was, she said "a very good friend". My mother had probably been meeting with him secretly on other occasions. There were a few other visits to the park when my mother and I met up with this man. Each time it was the same sort of experience. On each occasion I was reminded not to mention this secret tryst to anyone.

Then my grandfather died, and we continued living in the house, but my mother's brother and his family also moved into the house as the house was left to him by my grandfather. We were allowed to stay on.

Out of the blue one day when I was about 11 or 12 years old my mother told us that our father bought a house in a different suburb, and we were all going to live together in the new house. What father? I never knew we had one. My brother and sister, of course, knew about him and remembered him, but this sounded like a fairy tale to me.

However, we now lived together as a family, and I got to really learn about the stranger in our new house. Imagine realizing for the first time at the age of twelve that you have a father! It was hard to believe! He was kind, gentle and did whatever he could for us. He was the hardest working man I had ever seen. He woke up at about six in the morning, and took the tram to work. Due to the circumstances of his life he never owned a car or learnt to drive one. He worked six days a week until about eight or nine o'clock at night when he came home and had dinner. He took no lunch breaks or any other type of break. He spent Sundays at home doing paper-work for his store, such as check- writing and attending to business matters. He never went to the movies or visited family members with us, probably because he felt uncomfortable in their presence due to his history with them in the past. Their rejections of him were still painful. His life was his work, and his goal was to provide for his family. I did not spend much time with him as he was always working and, at this stage, I was in my teen-age years going out with friends and involved in sports.

On Saturdays I would go to my father's store, and try to help him out with some work there, as Saturday was the busiest day in the week when his store was teeming with customers. The miners did not work on that day, and instead, went shopping. It was also the day when many thefts took place on account of the store being so full of people. Another pair of eyes was always useful to detect the robbers. They would often send my father up a tall ladder to pick out an article sitting on a shelf just below the ceiling. While my father was climbing the ladder to retrieve the article, some of them would fill up their bags with goods within their reach. Little Big Eyes – that was me – was watching them. When my father came down the ladder, I would immediately report to him. He would physically remove his articles from their bags, and oust them from the store. This probably was the cause of some physical attacks that he was subjected to on his way home from work or going to the bank.

Then I was gone. At the age of sixteen I went off to college and, later, Medical School in Cape Town, a thousand miles away. And I never lived at home again, except for the occasions when I returned to Johannesburg for short vacations or to see my family. My father paid for my Medical School studies and the accommodation that went with it, even though he could scarcely afford it. I had only lived with my father for a period of five or six years. He was a man who gave a great deal and received very little. He asked for nothing, and was satisfied with what he had. He was a simple and honest person. His world was his family. He had had so little of them in the past that he seemed to be trying to make up for lost time. He only gave love, and wanted us all to be happy and content, and to lack nothing.

After I graduated from Cape Town University, I came to work fairly close to Johannesburg, and I was able to visit my parents about once per week. In the fullness of time, I married a young lady, Gladys, who came from New York, where she was born. Before we married, my father told her that he was unhappy about our forthcoming marriage. She asked him why that was so. He said to her "You are American. You are going to take my son away to America, and I do not wish to lose him."

She replied "I love this country more than America. I will never leave this country. You can rest assured that we will always live here and we will always be close to you". We continued to live in South Africa for about six years.

One day after receiving mail from New York Gladys said to me "I think we have to go to New York for about a year. My mother is developing dementia, my brother has had a stroke and a heart attack, and my sister is on the brink of divorce. We need to go and help them, and then we can return to South Africa."

We packed up our children, at that stage there were three of them under the age of four, and we went to live in New York. I found a job at Mount Sinai hospital, and we did as much as we could to assist her family in their problems. However, after one year her family problems had worsened, and we decided to stay in New York permanently. Our kids were getting used to their pre-school activities and friends and I was becoming more involved in my work.

I never realized at that time, how much our permanent re-location to New York had affected my father. Years later, after my wife Gladys died and I was cleaning out her drawers, I found a letter from my father written to her. She never mentioned it to me. He told her how disappointed he was in her for not sticking to her word when she said that she would never leave South Africa. "You have taken my son away from us and left us with no one to turn to, to help us in our old age". At this stage, my sister was married, and had a child of her own, my brother was of very little help to my parents because of his cerebral palsy. My parents were alone.

No life lives forever. Nobody knows what tomorrow will bring. Further tragedy was about to strike. My mother developed atrial fibrillation. Treatment for atrial fibrillation in those days was not what it is today. She soon had a stroke, became unconscious and died. I flew in from New York just in time to be with her living body but unconscious mind. I stayed for the funeral. Soon after I returned to New York my sister felt a lump in her breast. This was followed by surgery and chemotherapy. Neither was treatment then as good as it is today. She was dead in six months. My father could not take these two tragedies, one following about six months after the other - and a son with cerebral palsy and another lost in the jungles of New York. Within a year after my mother's passing, I received a phone call one morning while I was in the shower before going off to work. I jumped out of the shower, water dripping off my body, and managed to get to the phone. It was my cousin Ralph from Johannesburg.

"I am sorry to tell you, but your father passed away during the night."
I wish I had spent more time with him. I hardly ever got to know him.
People asked me "What was the cause of your father's death?"
"I think he died of a broken heart."
"You can't mean that. You're a doctor!"
"I think he died of a broken heart."

THOUGHTS ON RELIGION

There are those who will believe every word they read in a religious text and there are those who will believe nothing. In between, there are many grades of believers. Here is one.

Jesus, we are told, is the son of God. His mother was the Virgin Mary. Well, Virgin is the wrong word. It is from an incorrect translation of the Hebrew word 'ha-almah', which does not mean virgin. It translates as 'a young woman'. The Hebrew word for virgin is 'bethulah', and it does not appear anywhere in the text referring to Jesus' mother. Mary was a young married woman who had not yet become a mother – ha-almah. Apparently, when the Greeks were told about this error in the translation of 'ha-almah' (described as an epic error) they did not wish to do anything about changing it. Mary was married to Joseph, but we are told that he was not the father of Jesus. The father, it is said, was the Lord God (Mary was impregnated by the Holy Spirit), even though the Gospels of Matthew and Luke state that the father was Saint Joseph, Mary's husband. Were Matthew and Luke wrong in thinking that Joseph was the father, or did they just mean father figure – and not biological father? It is also said that Jesus came from the line of King David. If Jesus was the son of God he could not have come from the line of King David, since God did not come from the line of King David, and King David did not come from the line of God. Did Mary, the mother of Jesus, perhaps come from the line of King David? Unlikely, as Biblical Jews placed little importance upon women's lineage or where they came from.

The Catholic Church refers to Mary, mother of Jesus, as an eternal virgin. Yet we know that Jesus had four brothers – Joseph, James, Jude and

Simon – and two sisters – Salome and Mary. If Mary, mother of Jesus, was an eternal virgin, there is no mention that the Holy Spirit fathered all those children. Perhaps they were half-bothers and half-sisters to Jesus. The Catholic Church tries to explain this away by saying that there is no word in Aramaic, the language spoken in the time of Jesus, for cousin; so, they may be cousins, and not siblings. Also, they say that the Bible often refers to good friends as brothers even though they are not biological brothers.

Then again, according to Celsus, who lived in the second century A.D. and was a Roman writer who wrote in Greek (most intellectual Romans wrote in Greek), the true father of Jesus was Abdes Panthera who came into the Roman Empire from outside as a slave. He was later placed in the Roman army where he served for forty years, adding the Roman names of Tiberius and Julius to Abdes Panthera. At one stage he was transferred to Sidon in Northern Israel, not far from Nazareth, where he came across Mary and impregnated her. Apparently, Joseph was already married to her, and was about to leave her because of the adultery in which she had participated, but felt sorry for her predicament and the poor reputation that she would be bound to suffer if she would have had a child without a husband. He therefore stayed with her in order to protect her image. The Jerusalem Talmud also refers to the father of Jesus as being Panthera, a Roman soldier.

The Gospel of Matthew states that in a dream Joseph heard that King Herod was intending to kill the infant Jesus, because he had heard that the Magi had predicted that he would become King of the Jews, and Herod wanted no rivals. Therefore, we are told, that Joseph and Mary took the infant Jesus and fled to Egypt, which was beyond any territory controlled by Herod. Here they spent a total of two years, returning to Judea after the death of Herod. It appears as though Herod's successor was even more cruel, so they went north to Nazareth, far from his reach. We know nothing of the early life of Jesus until we hear of him being a young man and a rabbi. Some have made a case that he went to India and studied Buddhism in the north of India, in the Himalayas close to Nepal. It seems very strange that God's son would be interested in studying some other god-less religion. It distracts from the monotheistic beliefs which are central to the Hebrew religion. Buddhism is more like a philosophy, and does not seem to have any God at all.

During his life Jesus led an ideal and exemplary existence. He helped the poor, the weak and the sick. He cured those who were suffering and performed many magical acts. "A camel may pass through an eye of a needle easier than a rich man could go to Heaven," said Jesus. Like a camel, he would have to off-load a lot of material before even attempting to pass through a needle's eye. Did he learn all this in India? Whatever he said and did in his short life-time were examples of the life of a wonderful person. He made one error as far as I can remember, and that was when he was hungry while on his way to Jerusalem with his followers, and he found that the fig tree had produced no figs, whereupon he cursed the tree! That sounds far too human, and is not expected from the son of God who is all-knowledgeable and full of understanding. However, the Gospels have interpreted the incident otherwise. The Gospels say it was more of a parable. He was annoyed about the Jews at the Temple who would not listen to him. He was really saying that Jerusalem would fall and the Jews would come to an end. You shall be withered like a tree and not bear fruit.

After Pontius Pilate, the governor of the outpost of the Roman Empire which was named Palestine by the Romans, ordered him to be put to death on the crucifix, the act was performed. Pontius Pilate proposed the crucifix because Jesus' actions must have collided with the Roman authorities, since crucifixion was only reserved for the worst crimes and offences. Why was he put to death? Neither the Pharisees nor the Sadducees were in favor of his treatment of them, his over-turning of the tables of the money exchangers outside the Temple, and his very different approach to the handling of the people's problems. He frequently acted as though he were God – and even claimed to be God. He was accused of blasphemy and taken to Pontius Pilate amid the roars of a howling mob.

At the end of the day which was the beginning of the Jewish Sabbath he was removed from the crucifix and was declared dead. He was placed in a cave before the Sabbath arrived as nothing could be done with his body on the day of rest. Apparently, after death, he escaped, and on the fortieth day thereafter he ascended to Heaven. This is the act which ensured his place for posterity as the central figure in Christianity. Did some people steal the body? Was the body hidden? Did he go to Heaven? It is better not to know, because without the passage to Heaven there is no religion called Christianity!

Supposedly, the Bible treats all people equally because we are all God's children, and He loves us all dearly. Yet when Moses led the Jews out of Egypt and they had barely crossed the Red Sea they were confronted by the Amalekites at Rephidim in the Sinai Peninsula. In Exodus 17: 8-13 God called on Israel to exterminate the Amalekites (who were also God's children). Why did He create them bad or allow them to get bad? The Chosen People slayed as many as they could. Amalekites have been considered the arch- enemy of the Jews ever since then. Anti-Semites, such as Kmielnieki in Poland, Titus in Rome, Torquemada in Spain, Hitler in Germany, and many others have been referred to as Amalekites. Amalek was the grand-son of Esau who was the twin brother of Jacob, and who ran away into the desert harboring a hatred for his brother, Jacob (who had bought his birthright).

Slave-owners in the United States sometimes justified slavery by saying that their slaves were the Children of Ham who were cursed by God. Ham was the first son of Noah. One day, Ham saw his father sleeping while he was in the nude. Ham called upon his brethren to come and witness this strange and supposedly laughable sight. The brothers all walked in backwards so as not to observe their father's nudity. God recognized the action of the brothers to be correct and honorable towards their father, but Ham's behavior was considered to be ugly and immoral, unworthy of a son towards his father. To witness a father's naked body was looked upon as an incestuous homosexual act. God cursed Ham and all the generations following him. Thus, some slave-owners in America felt that their slaves were the Children of Ham, and deserved slave status as a result of the sins of their father.

Incest occurred once again in the Bible when Lot's daughters had sex with Lot, their father. After the events at Sodom and Gomorrah when Lot's wife was turned into a pillar of salt, Lot and his two daughters went to live in a cave close to the Jordan River. It was very lonely there and there were few men around for the two daughters to meet and to marry. God had said unto Abraham "Be fruitful and multiply". But it was not possible for these girls to observe God's will, so on separate occasions each daughter made her father drunk, and had sex with him. The incestuous relationships led to the births of Moab and Ben Ami, resulting in the tribes of Moabites and

Ammonites; and God cursed them and all their succeeding generations because they were born of incest.

Neither the Old Testament nor the New Testament give much credit to women. After creating the world and man and the animals, God decided after many years as an afterthought, that women are necessary for companionship. So, he created woman from Adam's rib while he was sleeping – not as an equal, but as a comrade and to obey her man. Perhaps, some have suggested, Adam had been created originally as a hermaphrodite, and when God later wished to create a woman, he took the female side out of Adam's body (called a rib in the Bible) and fashioned a woman as a companion for the male part that was still Adam. Adam's name comes from 'adamah' which means 'earth', and Eve is said to have been created as an 'ezer' which is Hebrew for 'helper'. She does not sound like an equal partner.

The lesser status granted to women in the Bible is obviously displayed. Lot's wife, an important person, who had been turned into a pillar of salt for turning around to witness the destruction of Sodom and Gomorrah where some of her children had lost their lives (who can blame a woman for turning around when her children are burning in the flames?), remains nameless. Lot's daughters are also nameless, despite the fact that they are the creators of the Moabite and Ammonite tribes. Surely tribal creators warrant a name disclosure, as would have occurred if they had been men!

Some individual, who had a great deal of spare time, counted the names in the Bible. He found thousands of men's names but just over a hundred names for women. Most of the women were not considered to be important enough to have their names mentioned. When a young Jewish lad has had his barmitzvah and he is considered an adult, he will perform the ritual daily prayer and announce every morning "Thank God that I was not born a woman".

When God made a covenant with Abraham so that the Children of Israel would become His Chosen People, the contract only referred to men. God claimed that all men of Israel were to be circumcised, and he that is not circumcised must be cast out from amongst his people. There is no contract for the women - no prayers, no special requirements, no signs of distinction. The religion appeared to be for men only. We are told in the chapters on Saul that women were good for preparing food, for taking care of their men, and for grieving. This appears to be a man's world – man is stronger and goes to war. However, women of the Bible are considered to be more knowledgeable, and often they were able to give their men advice and make them do what they wished them to do. The men were frequently told not to marry alien women as they often drag the men to live in the countries of their birth and make them pray to their gods, or they bring their alien gods and idols with them and force their husbands to worship them. Obviously, this was unwanted by the God of Israel.

When a man was found to have raped a woman, he was to pay a certain amount of silver to her father for having insulted him by committing this act upon his daughter. There was no requirement for an apology to the woman who was raped. In fact, the guilty man would be required to marry the daughter and live with her forever, despite any of her pleas demanding the contrary.

The Ten Commandments were written for men. One Commandment states that thou shalt not covet thy neighbor's wife. By doing so you will have offended your neighbor – not his wife, the woman who was coveted. There is no mention of coveting your neighbor's husband.

If a woman had a male child the Bible states that she bore her husband a son. There is no mention in the Bible of a woman bearing her husband a daughter. In Jeremiah 44:24 it states "I said to all the people and all the women". Apparently, men are people and women are something else. The Bible is dominated by men and was almost certainly written by men.

It states in the Bible that Moses was not circumcised. That is understandable, as after he was born, he had to be hidden to escape killing of the first-born of Jewish babies, as ordered by Pharaoh. Then he was put in a basket sealed with bitumen, placed on the River Nile and found by Pharaoh's daughter, who brought him to the palace where he lived until he was a grown man. There certainly were no facilities in Pharaoh's palace for the circumcision of Jewish boys. Thus, an uncircumcised Moses, according to the Old Testament, was not Jewish. In later verses in the Bible, it is related that Moses viewed the Burning Bush which did not consume itself, and from the Bush came the command from the Lord to take out the slaves from Egypt and deliver them to the Holy Land. Then, apparently, God realized that he had erred as Moses was uncircumcised. Zipporah who was not Jewish – she was a Midianite, the daughter of Jethro - discovering that God wished to kill Moses for not being circumcised, circumcised her own son and placed the foreskin from her son upon Moses' belly while he was sleeping. She fooled the Lord, looking down from the heavens, into thinking that Moses was now circumcised. Thus, he was able to go to Egypt and rescue the slaves.

There are laws that were given by God and there are laws that were engineered by people. Religious Jews observe both God-given and man-made laws. There are a group of people, however, who said that they will only observe God's laws, but would not observe man-made laws which were not the words of God and only subsequently added to the religion by mere mortals. They are the Karaites who mostly live in Israel (currently about 40,000), the United States and Ukraine. They have been present in the diaspora ever since the destruction of the Temple in about 70 A.D. They are observant Jews who only listen to the word of God. In World War II the Karaites escaped Hitler's anti-Jewish destructive sweeps in the Ukraine. German officers questioned whether the Karaites should be sent to the death camps like the other Jews; they were told no, as they weren't Jews – which, of course, is incorrect.

Some Biblical scholars have said that the Jews of today are not all descendants of the ancestral slaves in Egypt. Throughout the Ages there have been additions by conversions, marriages and other means to the ranks of Judaism despite huge concurrent losses. Some scholars have maintained, and thus far there is not enough information to prove it, that the nation of Khazars, who lived between the Caspian and Black Seas, converted to Judaism after comparing all other available religions and deciding that Judaism seemed to be the best. These scholars say that Ashkenazi Jews of Europe are not descendants of the Jews who were slaves in Egypt, but are the offspring of the Khazars. Arthur Koestler has written about this in his book "The Thirteenth Tribe". Believe it or not, but this is probably grossly exaggerated or a myth.

Even after the Ten Commandments were handed down by God to Moses on Mount Sinai Jews were building a Golden Calf under the guidance of Aaron, the brother of Moses. The Jews in the Sinai Desert were basically henotheists – worshippers of many gods, even though Yahveh was considered to be the superior God. God frequently admonished the Jews for creating and worshipping idols. Muslims say that they (Muslims) are God's

Chosen People. They admit that the Jew's had been His Chosen People in the past, but are no longer so because of their idol-worshipping. True monotheism only developed in Babylon after the Temple was destroyed by the Romans. Without a Temple and without a country of their own the Babylonian rabbis spent most of their time teaching and praying, and dissecting and digging deeper into hidden meanings in the Bible. They added many laws to which the Karaites later objected.

During the era of Greek domination of the Holy Land the Jews were greatly affected by the Hellenistic influence, especially in their philosophy. The Greeks had even encouraged them to write the Bible in Greek (the Septuagint), which was put together by a total of 72 members from the different tribes. Of course, the Greeks finally overplayed their role when they brought their idols into the Temple, and found themselves being attacked and defeated by the Maccabees. The offspring of the Maccabees were the Hasmoneans, who returned the leadership of the country to the Jews. They ruled from 165 B.C.E. but they ended their reign with a Civil War, and the anti-Hasmonean Jews appealed to Rome to come and save them, which they did in 63 B.C.E.

The Holy Land became an outpost of the Roman Empire. In 66 A.D. the Jews revolted against Roman rule. The Romans put an end to the revolt, destroyed the Temple and drove the Jews out of Judea. Without a Temple animal sacrifice came to an end. Jews relied on prayer as a replacement of animal sacrifice. The problem was how to receive atonement without a country and without a Temple. The rabbis preached and taught, and introduced Oral Law as an addition to the Bible, which became the Mishna and Gemorrah. The Oral Law was put into writing at a later date. Within those pages they learnt how to reach atonement and became monotheists.

Where does it say in the Bible that you are not permitted to eat milk products either with or after eating meat? It does not say so, but the rabbis introduced this law by attempting to explain the Biblical statement of "Thou shalt not seethe the kid in its mother's milk", a feature of Canaanite cooking where the baby goat was boiled in its mother's milk. Apparently, Jews had copied that culinary maneuver from the Canaanites. It seemed rather insensitive to boil the baby in its mother's milk, so the rabbis introduced dietary laws, separating meat and milk products so as to make meat-eating more humane.

Where does it say in the Bible that a Jew must have his head covered at prayer and wherever he goes (some even sleep with their heads covered)? It does not say that anywhere. Apparently when Moses ascended Mount Sinai to receive the Ten Commandments the light emanating from the Heavenly Presence was so intense that he had to cover his eyes. We obviously cannot walk around all day with our eyes covered while God is constantly present, so the next best thing is to have our heads covered – such was one of the rabbinical interpretations. Women cover their heads in respect of the men. Exposing one's hair might be looked upon as exposing a part of one's body, and therefore she could be considered as a woman with low morals.

Practicing Jews, especially Orthodox, will always encourage their children to marry within the Jewish faith; Reform Jews will be less strict about inter-marriage. Most, however, will be joyful as long as they think that their son or daughter is happy in his or her marriage. Others will never speak to that child again on account of the iniquitous act he or she had committed by marrying outside the Faith. There are some that will even sit shiva for the child (go into mourning, as for the dead) if such a marriage occurs. The Bible warns about marriage to non-Jews and foreign women, who will bring their idols into the house and make their husbands worship their gods. They may even take their Jewish husbands to live in their own land and force their gods upon them there. Yet many of our Biblical heroes have married foreign women. Moses, our leader, who delivered the Jewish slaves from Egypt to the Holy Land, married Zipporah, a Midianite and the daughter of Jethro. The Midianites were Africans. Ruth, who was a Moabite (non-Jewish) married Boaz, and was probably an ancestor of King David. King Solomon had numerous wives, most of whom were non-Jewish and from foreign lands. Many kings of Israel and of Judea married foreigners. Samson met and was due to marry Delilah, a Phillistine. Samson was a very strong man, but she cut his hair, the source of his strength, and was responsible for his capture by the Philistines. Ahab, one of the kings of Israel, married Jezebel, a Phoenician princess, who forced him to worship Baal and her other gods. She was responsible for the deaths of many Hebrew prophets, which upset Elijah, who predicted that Ahab would be killed and Jezebel would be eaten by dogs. Elijah was correct – Ahab was killed, and Jezebel's fate was that she was trampled and then eaten by dogs.

In Europe during the Middle Ages and even up to the twentieth century Jews were living in ghettos and shtetls, and therefore associated mostly with other Jews while hardly ever meeting non-Jews. When they wished to marry, their only choices were amongst Jewish women living in the ghetto or shtetl. Today in America and also the rest of the world Jews are meeting non-Jews on the university campus, in business, at clubs and parties, on the sports fields and on the Internet. Increased contact will obviously create more mixed marriages, adding to the problems which might occur in marriages which cross inter-racial lines. Many of our children and grandchildren are being lost to Judaism, far more than had occurred in years gone by.

If you are a religious person, are you sure that you are believing in the right God? Because you are born in a Christian, Islamic or Jewish environment and you believe in a Christian, Islamic or Jewish God it does not mean that yours is the true deity. You only happened to have been born into a community where this particular deity was worshipped. What about the 1.2 billion people born in India and the 1.6 billion born in China or the Shintos of Japan or the Bahai of Iran or polytheists and idol-worshippers, who were all born into different communities? Are they all wrong about whom they worship, and only your God is the correct one? Your choice of God usually depends upon where you were nurtured and who encouraged you to participate in that particular religion. You might have been born in Timbuktu, where a different God might have been advertised to you. I remember at school I felt that our sports teams were the best, and I had little good to say about the other schools' teams. Is my religion the best?

Fables associated with religion are numerous and not always believable. Methusaleh was supposed to have lived to almost a thousand years. The physiology of the human body would not allow such longevity, even with today's progress in medical advances. Perhaps when he was about one hundred he became senile and still had nine hundred years to go! Noah could not have built an Ark large enough to accommodate all the species of life in the world, two by two. Egyptian ancient history (which has been accurately recorded on papyrus) does not confirm that there was a Jewish conclave of slaves in the land of the Pharaohs or that Moses performed a number of magic tricks, or that there were ten plagues and some people drowning in the Red Sea while others walked on dry land because the sea opened up for them. Try not to be carried away by miracles! There is no magic – only the magician knows the secret.

If God created heaven and earth, where was God during the Creation? Was he sitting on a chair? At that time no chairs existed. Was he sitting on a rock? It, too, had not been created yet – he only created rocks later. Was God inside or outside the world that He was going to create? There was no inside nor outside. Everything was a void. Oh, I am told by some, look upon God as a Spirit. Well in that case, I must be a whiff of wind or a spirit because I was created in God's image!

Perfect intelligent design is how the results of the Creation are described. Yes, there are wonders to be beheld as delivered by a perfect God, but there are many mistakes. Anatomy of the human body is not always perfect. God could have kept the esophagus a little further from the trachea so our dinners could not go the wrong way or allow inhalation of gastric contents from gastric reflux to occur. The reproductive system, too, could have been a little further away from the excretory systems. Infections and diseases have spread throughout mankind through the ages. I am not complaining, but it does not fit in well with Perfect intelligent design. Volcanoes, hurricanes, earthquakes, floods and droughts have ravaged civilizations ever since the Creation. Why does God allow evil? Do the unevangelized suffer harsher punishment than the believers? Stephen Hawking says Hell contradicts God's benevolence.

Richard Dawkins, a noted atheist, said that we are all atheists as far as belief in all of the gods in ancient history are concerned, but we atheists just go one God further. True, nobody believes in Zeus and Thor and the ancient Egyptian gods any more. The theist has eliminated all gods, except the God in which he believes, the others being false. Blind faith eliminates thought and discourages exploration and inquiry. Religious belief is protected through the power and wealth of religious institutions – churches, temples and mosques.

Is there no Heaven for the inhabitants of Papua, New Guinea or Kiribati in Oceania? We are told that one must be a Christian in order to go to Heaven. What happens to people who have not been born Christian or have not been offered Baptism or the opportunity to follow Jesus? Why are some people sent to Hell (we are told) when they are considered to be evil? Why does a baby with no knowledge of evil sometimes die? And why do some criminals or people who rob and cheat in business often lead happy and comfortable lives?

Some have said that without religion there could be no morality or ethical behavior. The Bible, they say, teaches us how to behave towards all those with whom we come into contact. Did our ancestors lack morality before the days that the Bible was written? Morality preceded the Old Testament by thousands of years. Man belongs to the family of Primates, the same family to which the apes and gorillas and chimpanzees belong. We all have seen altruism in these and other animals. We have seen apes help other wounded apes traverse the jungles and we have noticed their sensitivity to emotions of hurt or sick members of their troops or groups. I certainly think that humans are endowed with a sense of morality, even when there is an absence of religion. We know that religion does not always teach you the right thing? We have read in the Bible of the actions by the Creator displaying misogyny (the status of women), homophobia, racism (slaying of the Amalekites), genocide (the Ten Plagues), ethnic cleansing (Sodom and Gemorrah). We have seen the innocents die as a result of tsunamis, hurricanes, tornadoes, floods and droughts.

On 9/11/2001 New York City's Twin Towers were hit by Muslims, mostly from Saudi Arabia, in order to carry out the wish of their God, Allah. Almost three thousand people were killed (this included an attack on the Pentagon) on this day. Their belief was that they would spend an eternity in Paradise, amidst a large number of virgins, and remain heroes of Allah forever. This information was given to them by the Holy Koran. Is this an example of morality from religious teachings? Does Allah applaud the destruction of three thousand people?

In Genesis Abraham is ordered by God to prepare his child for his murder and his sacrifice to God. Abraham does not argue, but follows God's command. Later God said "Spare the child. Sacrifice an animal to me instead." Did Abraham behave correctly in carrying out God's order or should he have argued or asked questions? This was blind faith, displaying no reasonable thought. I would not give Abraham good grades for his indifference to the life of his child despite his trust in the Lord. Morality in religion is presented as dogma. The atheist or agnostic employs reason in accepting morality as a virtue. According to the Bible, a leper, must be taken outside the city gates, and we must "stone her" – this also applies to an adulterous woman while the murderer and the business man who produces Ponzi schemes continues to live to a ripe old age! When a President talks of grabbing women and man-handling them and his ecclesiastical supporters cheer him and vote for him, is this morality?

God told the Hebrews escaping from the Egyptians in the Sinai Desert to kill all the Amalekites, His own children whom he had created. They must have been really bad to necessitate such a fate! The Crusaders waged religious wars against the infidels in order to wrest the religious places for Christians in the Holy Land. I thought the Jews were his Chosen People and that the Holy Land was for them. The Pope's armies fought many religious wars in Europe through the centuries; this is rather a severe form of aggression from the Pope who represents God on earth. "Thou shalt not kill." The Spanish Inquisition of 1492 was a Catholic promulgation to kill Jews and Muslims who did not convert to Christianity. For almost two thousand years the Catholics have accused the Jews of being Christ killers. I thought Pontius Pilate gave the order to crucify! Slavery was not considered immoral, but homosexuality was. All this is very confusing in the presence of a loving and moral Creator. Surely, rationality in morality and ethics makes more sense than blind faith.

Jesus said that everyone who asks will receive, everyone who seeks will find, he who prays will have his prayers answered. Has that been your experience? Have there been times when your prayers were not answered? Or is this another fairy tale like Santa Claus or the Tooth Fairy? Don't you think that we should have more evidence of proof before we accept these tales? The Bible is a Book written by man. It contains primitive man's own beliefs and superstitions, while many stories have been plagiarized (like the Book of Esther taken from children's stories in Persian books), and the life of Moses which emulates the life of Sargon who lived in Mesopotamia a thousand years before Moses, who was placed in a basket and was floated down a river, saved by a woman, and became a great leader of his people. It is good to worship heroes even if they have been stolen from elsewhere!

My dictionary defines religion as worship or belief in a super-human controlling power. It describes superstition as excessive belief in supernatural control. They both sound pretty similar to me.

Religious people seem to think that faith is the most important attribute for man. Faith is belief without thought. Faith is belief without the backing of science and reason. Voltaire said that those who can make us believe in absurdities can make us commit atrocities. Richard Dawkins said that faith can be dangerous; don't implant it into an innocent child! Faith teaches you to stop thinking, questioning – just accept and be satisfied. Another atheist, Christopher Hitchens said "A virgin can conceive. A dead man can walk again. A leper can be cured (before the days of modern medicine). The blind can see again. It is not moral to lie to children."

We don't have much faith in the intellectual powers of primitive man. He had little learning and no knowledge of science. He believed in superstitions and dreams and guidance from dead ancestors – that was his dogma. Why are we so willing to accept his thoughts and words about God when we accept no other of his primitive beliefs?

TIERS IN SOCIETY

$\mathcal{I}$ could have misspelled the word and called this chapter 'Tears in society'. The title would have been equally apt.

The Bible tells us that we are all God's children. He loves us all the same. Jesus loved all the people, and he was particularly attentive and kind to the poor, the lame, prostitutes and those to whom life had been a burden. However, people, including many of the followers of Jesus, the wealthy and religious, are not as loving to their fellow travelers as was Jesus. In fact, all around us we see examples of man's inhumanity to man.

If I were a person with a black skin living in Africa I might have been sold to a slave-owner in the southern part of the United States, and worked on his cotton fields for the lowest of wages, and my children and grand-children would also have been owned by the cotton farmer, worked as a slave for him, too, or sold to his neighbor who needed more help on his farm. My wife, too, would belong to my owner, and, as his property, he could do with her whatever he wished – he could even sell her to someone else and leave me alone!

If I were a black man living in South Africa before 1990, I would not have been a slave and I would not have been bought or been the property of a white man, but I would have been living under the laws of a government that treated me as sub-human. My work would have been a necessary contribution to the financial strength of my employer and the country. I might have been working on the gold mines or in construction, but I would have been paid a pittance. I would be living in sub-standard housing. I would not be allowed into restaurants, theaters or places of entertainment, and, in fact, I would not even have been allowed to go on the streets unless

I had a note from my employer giving me permission to be present in a certain area until a certain time. Jail would be my destination if I broke those rules.

If I were born into the Dalit caste (Untouchables) in India, I would be treated with no respect. For me there would be no education, only menial and dirty tasks. Somebody has to take animal corpses off the street and attend to dead human remains. Nobody wants to do such work, so it would be up to me to do it. I would be oppressed and attacked. I would be robbed of access to education and of general improvement to my living standards. Nor does anyone want to touch an Untouchable, like me. In fact, I would have to clean up my own footprints, so everything should remain pure and uncontaminated for those fortunate enough to have been born into higher castes than mine. Untouchables should ring a bell when approaching, so that all would be aware of their imminence. Dalits (meaning 'oppressed') committing a minor crime may receive a death sentence or jail, but an upper caste member would receive minimum penalties or none at all for a similar crime. Low caste members can never graduate from their lowly status.

Karma is a religious doctrine which states that an individual's place in society is pre-determined by his past life. You must remain in your caste and cannot change it. In 1950 after India received independence the Dalits and other op pressed castes were promised equal rights, equal educational opportunities and access to financial possibilities. However, it is difficult to overcome entrenched societal habits and rites, so that the situation does not seem to have altered very much.

It is not only in India, South Africa and the southern states of the U.S.A. where the lowest castes have had to do all the dirty work. This also occurs in many other countries of the world. Japan is another example of a land where the lowest classes were doing the filthiest work. From your address it could be told if you were from a low class, whereupon your address could be a license to discriminate against you. In 1871 the caste system was abolished in Japan, but even today there appears to be remnants of this old custom being maintained to a certain extent. The low castes in Japan are the Burakumin (hamlet people) and the Eta (full of filth). The Samurai were the warrior class, and once dominated Japan. They were considered on a par with the nobility. They married with their own people. Some Samurai women were warriors, too.

Pakistan became a self-governing country after the division of India following World War II. As in India, the country consists of Hindus and Muslims. Islam prides itself as being a religion where the lowliest people are equal to the emirs and princes in the eyes of the Lord. However, the Hindus of Pakistan follow the same caste system as their brethren in India.

Jews have been living in Germany since before the Middle Ages and have fought for Prussia and the German states in their wars, including World War I. They made numerous contributions to medicine, the sciences, philosophy and culture in Germany. However, after the first World War Adolph Hitler was elected to leadership, and later increased his own power even further. He developed a hatred for the Jew before he became the Fuhrer. He drove them out of their professions and made their lives miserable. He blamed them for the ills of Germany. He blamed them for the loss of World War I and he blamed them for an attempted communist coup in the Weimar Republic (post-war Germany). He ranted against the contamination of the German people caused by the inferior non-Aryan Jews (his words), and decided that this pestilence must be expunged. He planned the extinction of the entire Jewish race. He placed them on the lowest rung of German society, and by the end of the second World War he was responsible for the deaths of six million Jews from German and European society – apart from creating millions of refugees, who fled in order to save their lives.

In concentration camps, stripped of their own clothes and forced to wear uniform pajama-like garb, they were also stripped of their names and granted tattooed numbers on their arms. Personal identity was exchanged for being an element of a large ugly mob.

A scapegoat is a person or a group of people who are singled out for blame for the faults, failures or unpleasant tidings that occur to society. The scapegoat is seldom deserving of blame, but it takes the pressure off society. The term is derived from the goat in the Bible that was chosen by the High Priest on Yom Kippur to carry all the sins of the people, and sent away into the desert.

People on the lower rungs of society are frequently scapegoated for the ills in their society. Jews are not strangers to being the scapegoats of the people of Europe. They have been blamed for epidemics in the past and for killing Christian children so that they could use their blood for the production of matzos for Passover. Both of these examples are obvious lies, but the higher classes believed these accusations, even though they are irrational.

Throughout the world we can find examples of people who are treated as less than people – somewhere between an animal and a person - by their fellow-countrymen. Skin color is a common cause of race hatred, because it is so easy to identify. However, hatred for a section of the population could also be arrived at as a result of other physical defects, either handed down or acquired. In the case of anti-Semitism there are no physical differences of Jews from the general population, but there may be a difference in attire or their easily-recognized elongated locks attached to the scalp, or their highly developed business acumen could cause them to be easily recognized. There could also be a jealousy for their intellectual prowess in philosophy, medicine, science and education.

There is the problem, too, of the way you believe in God, even though the three major monotheistic religions believe in the same God. Some religious groups might not like the way in which you pray to Him (the same God). Muslims dislike the fact that Jews call themselves the Chosen People. They say they are the Chosen People now, having replaced the Jews for their idolatry in Biblical days. Islamic devotees deny that the Alawites of Syria are Muslim because they include some Christian practices in their devotion, and say that they are polytheists, like the Christians, who pray to God, Jesus, Mary and some of their Saints. Christians have persecuted Jews for two thousand years because they called the Jews Christ-killers. We all know that the order for the crucifixion of Jesus was given by Pontius Pilate, the Roman governor of Palestine. Christ was a Jew, and never gave up on his Judaism. It was Christ's followers who gave up on Judaism. "I have not come to change my Faith one jot or tittle"

Mohammed created his religion of Islam, based on Judaism, but when Jews and Christians were living in Arab and other Muslim countries, they were forced to pay a dhimmi for being non-Muslims, praying to the same God. Dhimmi was a tax. They, too, had to remain insignificant and wear a badge so that all would know of their inferiority.

It has been said on many occasions by numerous people that Israel is an apartheid society. They make that statement because of their opinion of the way that Palestinians are being treated by the Israeli government. They feel that the Palestinians living in Israel are living as a lower caste. Well, it is a ridiculous remark because it is made without any knowledge of what apartheid consisted of. Palestinians in Israel have an equal vote to all Jewish residents. Under the government in South Africa no Black man ever voted until the day that the apartheid government was thrown out of power at the end of the 20th century. No Black person in South Africa was ever allowed to serve in the government. In Israel there are no laws barring Palestinians from government service. In fact, there are Palestinians in the Israeli administration. In South Africa Blacks were not allowed to attend restaurants, theaters or any entertainment areas reserved for Whites. This is not the case for Palestinians in Israel, nor are there pass laws in Israel. Some people spread false information which can only be called lies, which are to the detriment of the true situation.

Society has divided its people into roughly three divisions. The Upper Class – the elite, the wealthy and those with power; the Middle Class – the non-manual workers, the educated, the doctors and lawyers; and the Working Class – the manual worker with lower educational standards. Social classes impact families, as well as the lives and opportunities of their people unless they can escape from their class. Escape is not easy because for that one would require financial aid and/or education which itself requires money. In many parts of the world, one would have to change the color of his or her skin, or the family history.

How far back does discrimination amongst classes of people go? We can go back to the Old Testament and read the story of Moses. We know that he married a Midianite – Zipporah (meaning 'bird'), the daughter of Jethro – when he ran away from Pharoah's Palace after killing an Egyptian. The Midianites are often referred to as the people from Kush. Kush is in Africa, probably in the region of Ethiopia of today. They are Black. Thus, Zipporah was a Black woman. Aaron and Miriam were the siblings of Moses, and they chided him for marrying a Black woman. We cannot be sure, but the nagging might have been because he married an alien woman. Nevertheless, apparently the criticism was mainly from Miriam. The Bible states that God punished Miriam with leprosy, as white as snow – opposite to the color of the skin of Zipporah.

29

The division of society into different tiers is known as social stratification, and it is affected by race, gender, sexuality and nationality. This, in turn, affects our occupation, degree and type of education, and our incomes. It also is responsible for our unequal access to rights and resources, and ultimately to power. Without equal rights we cannot all receive the best education and the best development in our businesses and occupations. Different tiers allow us different maximal goals.

Constitution of the United States is a liberal document and admired by most people. "All men are created equal", it states, but by that it really means "All White Protestant landowner males are created equal". Jefferson, the main architect, and most of the co-signors had a large number of slaves who were far from equal in status to Jefferson and other White men. Jefferson (and Lincoln) believed that Black people did not have the intelligence of Whites, nor could they be relied upon to vote. There are huge gaps between Black and White wage-earners even today, also between males and females doing the same work, and between the rich and the poor.

African slaves had been coming to America ever since the Portuguese navigators captured and brought them from Angola towards the beginning of the seventeenth century. The Catholic Church had decided that the Portuguese would have control over Africa and the East while Spain would be responsible for developing the New World. African slave labor turned out to be a great help for the Southern farmers in America, working on the crops of cotton, tobacco and all fruits and vegetables. They owned their slaves, and they owned the slave's families. They were not permitted to learn to read or write. They were under curfew every night and were not allowed to leave the property without permission. Nor could they testify in court against a White person. In order to marry they required permission from their employer. In fact, they had no rights.

The Founding Fathers had actually decided to cease the importation of African slave labor in 1808, but unfortunately for them Eli Whitney discovered the cotton gin at that time. This actually made work on the cotton plants easier, but because of the cotton gin more people entered into cotton planting and growing which necessitated more labor, and thus the need for more slaves.

At the end of the Civil War the Proclamation of the Emancipation of Slavery was issued by Lincoln in January, 1863. Some slaves, who were afraid that they might not be able to handle the exigencies of freedom, preferred not to go anywhere and remained in the employ of their previous owners for a small wage. Northerners were afraid that they would be inundated by the slaves wishing to get out of the South. Republicans felt that the slaves received too little freedom and Democrats felt that they received too much freedom from the Emancipation. All in all, it was difficult for most of the slaves who would have to start a new life with no education, no money and a hostile White background.

After the Emancipation Proclamation, there followed a period of Reconstruction. Blacks in the South were living in poverty, perhaps even worse than during slavery, when at least they were fed and had a place to live. Jobs were difficult to attain as their state of slavery did not permit them to get any education. There was no compensation paid out to slaves when they were freed, and White prejudice persisted. At least, the brutality and torture of slavery had come to an end. Yet, they found that they could not sit on juries, were not permitted to serve in the army and were not allowed to testify against Whites. They had won some freedom, but there was much still to be achieved.

The Jim Crow Era commenced after the Civil War and did not end until 1968 – over a hundred years. What the Federal government had granted to the slaves, the Southern state governments were intent on removing. The 15th Amendment had granted freed slaves the right to vote. However, this right was denied by the states. Education and decent jobs, too, were denied to them. Those who defied Jim Crow laws were tortured and jailed. The state's Black Codes were local laws which told ex-slaves where they could work and where they were permitted to reside. Once imprisoned they were treated as slaves. The courts inflicted more severe sentences upon ex-slaves than upon the general population. Jim Crow laws were not unlike the apartheid laws of South Africa which were developed almost one hundred years later – separate restaurants, theaters, water fountains, queues at banks and where people had to wait their turn. Segregation was enforced.

The Klu Klux Klan (KKK) was a hate organization that took the law into its own hands in order to terrorize Black people, burn down their schools and churches, and lynch them. Many Blacks died at their hands.

They were a terrorist organization, in today's vocabulary, with a set of their own rules. Nobody did much to control them while they caused fear and terror in the Black person's heart.

It was only in the middle of the 20th century that the lot of the African-Americans started to improve with the rise of the Civil Rights Movement. In 1948 President Harry Truman integrated the U.S. Army. Educational segregation was declared unconstitutional in 1954 as a result of the case of Brown v. Board of Education. In 1964 President Lyndon Johnson introduced the Civil Rights Act which formally ended segregation. Despite these Civil Rights laws it may still be difficult to guarantee that there is now equality in the U.S.

Ignorance and upbringing can cause one group of society to feel that they are better than another. Wealth and religion, too, might wish to separate the haves and the have nots, the clean and the unclean, God's chosen and God's cursed. Those with power might wish to force the weak in body and spirit into service for them or slavery. Basically, we are all homo sapiens. We all need food, work, oxygen and a heart-beat to stay alive. The rest is spice and garnish.

JEWS LIVING IN
ARAB LANDS

*J*ews have been living in Arab lands for millennia, ever since Biblical days and over a thousand years before Islam arrived. We read that Abraham left Ur in Mesopotamia and went to the land of Canaan at God's instructions after destroying the idols that were being sold in his father's store. He was a monotheist. It is estimated that was between 2000 and 1700 B.C.E. The first mention of Arabs is about 700 B.C.E. It therefore appears as though the Jews preceded the Arabs in the Middle East. Nevertheless, they have been living in close proximity for a long time. At times relationships have been good, whereas at other stages in history there have been killings, pogroms, forceful prevention of attempted departures and sometimes exile or loss of citizenship.

We hear so much about three-quarters of a million Palestinians who, before1948, had been living in the land that was taken over by Israel, and were either forced out of the country or became refugees as a result of fleeing for their freedom. They are still refugees today more than seventy years later. They have lived in encampments in Jordan, Lebanon and other neighboring Arab states, and have not been absorbed into the general populations of these countries – nor have they wanted to. Instead of 750,000 refugees we now have a few million as a result of the natural increase following childbirth over a period of seventy years. They are being subsidized by the United Nations and other donors, which has made the seeking of citizenship and the search for jobs less urgent for the Palestinian refugees. Their most urgent desire is to rid the Middle East of its Jews. They have received much sympathy for their plight.

However, we do not hear much about a larger number of Jews (at least 850,000) who were living in Arab lands before Israel became a nation and were driven out or forced to leave by their Arab hosts at the time of the inception of the state of Israel (before and after). There were no homeless Jewish refugees as a result of these forced departures. Unlike the Palestinian refugees, all were absorbed into Israel or other lands (like the U.S. and Canada), and made to feel at home in their new environment. They became integrated into their new communities, not leaving behind any refugee problem.

JEWS IN IRAQ

Diaspora refers to the dispersion of a people from their homeland. The word has frequently been associated with the spread of the Jews from their homeland ever since the days of the Bible. You will remember that the original Jewish Kingdom had split up into two kingdoms – Israel and Judah. In 750 B.C.E. the Assyrian army drove the Jews out of Israel and sent them into exile in Assyria. The offspring of those Jews no longer exist, and they are referred to today as the Ten Lost Tribes. There is evidence that those who did not assimilate with the local population and did not accept the local gods participated in a large diaspora lasting numerous decades which took them to Africa, India, China and, perhaps, Japan.

One hundred and fifty years later we witnessed a similar diaspora - the Babylonian exile. In 584 B.C.E. the Babylonians under Nebuchadnezzar conquered Judah and destroyed the Temple. They sent most of the Jews to live in Babylon, so that there were more Jews living in Babylon than in Judah. It was the practice of the victors in those days to exile much of the population of the losers' country to the land of the winners in order for them to learn the ways of the winners, while the winners would send some of their own people to the losers' country in order to help re-build the newly won land in the style which they preferred.

Seventy years after the Babylonian exile, Babylon itself was conquered by Cyrus of Persia. He kindly gave permission to the captive Jews in Babylon to return to their homes in Judea, if they so desired. Only a minority of the Jews were willing to move back – about 50 thousand. Among them were Ezra and Nehemia. Ezra was responsible for the re-building of the Temple in Jerusalem, which was a historic event. The return to Zion did not happen again until the twentieth century – or about 2500 years later - after Zionism became a platform, culminating in 1948 into the State of Israel established by the United Nations.

The majority of Jews that stayed on in Babylon after the return of the minority to Judea could not have been too unhappy with Babylon, because despite a protected passage to the land of their birth they chose exile. I think they had faith in Cyrus. This was unlike the Jews who had been defeated and driven out from Israel by the Assyrians less than two hundred years before that, because they did not remain as Jews in Assyria. Why did the Babylonian Jews survive and contribute so much to Judaism while the Assyrian Jews have not been heard of ever since their expulsion?

Their homeland, the Temple in Jerusalem, animal sacrifice and other religious rites were no longer a part of the lives of the Babylonian Jews. They had to start to re-build their religious rituals all over again. Historically, Babylon was no stranger to the Jews since Abraham, the Father of the Jewish people was born in Ur, which is a part of Babylon. He had moved to the Holy Land many centuries before by obeying God's instructions.

Five hundred years later, at the time of the Roman control of the Jewish land, known to the Romans as Palestina (or Palestine), the Jewish population was increasing. There were Jews who had been left behind following the Assyrian and Babylonian occupations, as well as those who had returned with Ezra and Nehemia. Jews had been resisting the heavy hand of the Romans from about 66 C.E. The Romans put down a Jewish revolt in 70 C.E. and destroyed the re-built Temple for a second time. There was a continued Jewish resistance at Masada which the Romans overcame in 73 C.E. Again in 138 C.E. the Romans defeated the Palestinian Jews who were led this time by Bar Kochba, who was looked upon by some as the Messiah, in a revolt against them. These wars caused more Jews to flee to Babylon. Life in Babylon was good whereas the Jews in Palestine were being persecuted by the Romans. Prior to the Romans the Jews had been persecuted by the Greeks. In fact, the Jews were happy to see the Romans arriving and welcomed them after they took over the land from the Greeks, as they thought the Romans would allow them more freedom; but it was not to be!

Babylon became the center of Judaism. The Jews of Babylon remained loyal citizens in their adopted land, saying "The law of the kingdom is our law". They still looked upon Jerusalem as the home of Judaism in the same way as Jews of the diaspora look upon Jerusalem today. Babylonian Jews did whatever they could to help their brethren in the Holy Land in their plight.

Between 300 to 500 C.E. the Babylon Talmud was composed and written. It consisted of texts, legends, commentaries and laws. The Babylonian Talmud was written about 100 years after the Jerusalem Talmud (which was actually written in Caesaria). The Babylonian Talmud takes precedence over the rarely used Jerusalem Talmud. The Gaon was the chief rabbi of the Jews in Babylon, and he always played an important role in religious observance. The Gaon led the discussions on religious commentaries and the teaching of the law. A different Gaon was responsible for the Jewish community and any social problems that may have arisen within the community. Some Jews broke away from the Babylonian Talmud because they did not wish to follow man-made laws. They would only accept God's words in the original Bible which was supposed to have been written by the hand of God. They are the Karaites who still exist today and live in Israel, the United States and the Caucasus.

Then the Muslims arrived in the 7th century, about 1300 years after the Jews had preceded them in Babylon (Iraq). The Jews lived under Muslim leadership while surviving through the dhimmi which was a sort of tax payable by non-Muslims for not being Muslims. They also had to display humility and show, in many ways, that they were not equal, but inferior, to Muslims. They were frequently required to wear a badge of distinction so that all would know who they were. When Benjamin of Tudela, a Spanish Jew who traveled the then-known world, came to Babylon in the 12th century, he said that there were about 40,000 Jews living there, mostly in good and prosperous conditions.

The population began sliding downwards because the Mongols invaded and took over control of everybody's lives towards the end of the 13th century and beginning of the 14th century. Many Jews left Babylon to escape the torture and destruction caused by the invaders. Following the Mongol invasion the Ottoman Empire spread into the Middle East, bringing back the Muslim religion and culture. The situation in Babylon further deteriorated because there was a continuing rivalry and struggle between Ottomans and Persians (even though the Persians, too had become Muslim), laying waste to the land.

However, in 1794 Babylonian Jewry underwent a renaissance. Synagogues were being re-built and added to, in Baghdad, the largest city in Iraq, and Jewish business acumen was coming to the fore. Baghdad was established in the 8th century and became the capital of the Abbasid Empire (Muslim). It was trading with much of Asia, from Singapore to China. British textiles were being exported to Iraq in large quantities, while Jewish traders were playing a major role in the increased international business which was arriving in the Middle East.

In 1917 the Ottoman Empire witnessed its last days, having chosen the wrong ally - it was on Germany's side in World War I. The Treaty of Versailles handed Iraq to Britain as a mandate. In 1932 Iraq became an independent country. The British had promised 'pay-back' to the Arabs for assisting them in the World War against the Ottoman Empire. One of King Faisel's sons was offered the post of monarch of Iraq, which he accepted. Jews were thriving in Iraq. However, nobody could have predicted the doom that was approaching.

At the same time Zionism was growing amongst the Jews throughout the world. Theodore Herzl, an Austrian secular Jew, a lawyer and writer, had decided that the Jews would never live peacefully and without fear from anti-Semitism unless they had their own land – and there was none better than their original Biblical home. "Next year in Jerusalem" became the rallying cry throughout international Judaism. It was less so in Iraq, however, as many Jews there were comfortable and considered themselves to be Communist. Zionism did not seem to go well together with Communism. Muslims, and especially Arabs, feared an impending national home for Jews in Palestine. Anti-Semitic riots broke out in Palestine and other Arab countries, including Iraq. These riots were called the Farhud in Baghdad. Hitler and his Nazi hordes spread anti-Jewish rhetoric and attacked Jews in Germany while encouraging people like the Grand Mufti of Jerusalem and other Middle Eastern potentates into activating anti-Semitic attacks, setting off rioting in Palestine, Iraq, Syria and Egypt.

After Israel became a State the government of Israel helped to deliver Iraqi Jews by many plane-loads into Israel. This was known as Operation Ezra and Nehemia. It occurred in 1951, whereby 130,000 Iraqi Jews out of a total of 150,000 were delivered back to Israel in numerous plane-loads after an extraordinary exodus having lasted over two thousand years in Babylon. Ezra and Nehemia were the two people who led the return to Judea for re-building the Jewish presence as well as the Jerusalem Temple when Cyrus permitted a return to the Holy Land from Babylon. Some Jews also went to the United States and other countries. There are three Jews left in Iraq at the time of writing.

JEWS IN EGYPT

Jews have been living in Egypt since the days of the Old Testament. Joseph was sold by his unfriendly and jealous brothers to some traders who took him off to Egypt. Due to his intelligence, he found himself working in Pharoah's court in a high position. Later when there was a famine in the land of Israel many Jews came to Egypt in order to seek food and shelter. Before long they became slaves unto Pharoah. It is even said that their labor was used to help build the pyramids. Archaeologists in Egypt, however, deny that Jews were ever slaves unto Pharaoh as no artefacts to that effect have ever been found. They also say that the Pyramids had already been constructed about one thousand years before the Jews were supposed to have arrived in Egypt (circum 1300 B.C.E.). It is also questionable whether Moses was a Jew. The Bible states that he was not circumcised. Moses is not a Jewish but an Egyptian name. We read in the Bible that after he was born, he was hidden by his mother, as Jewish newborn boys had been slated to be killed. Then he was placed in a basket sealed with bitumen and sent floating down the River Nile, whereupon he was found in the river by Pharoah's daughter who brought him back to the castle, where he grew up and became an adult. Obviously, there would not have been any circumcision in Pharoah's castle for Jewish boys. God had made a contract with Abraham that all Jewish boys would have to be circumcised, and that he who was not circumcised would not be a

Jew. One of the pharaohs of Egypt, Akhenaten, was a believer in one God, and even though monotheism was not a popular belief, he did have some following – perhaps Moses was one of them.

Apart from those Jews who had arrived in Egypt there was another group that arrived with Jeremiah. After the Babylonian conquest of Judea by Nebuchadnezzar and the exile of the Jews to Babylon, a small number of them were left in Judea under the control of a Jewish governor. This man was assassinated, and many of the remaining Jews, fearing for their lives, departed. Under Jeremiah, the Prophet, they fled to Egypt. Jeremiah probably spent the rest of his life in Egypt. He complained that Judea fell to the Babylonians because the Jews were punished by God for their idol worship.

In time Alexandria, a flourishing city, was developing a large Jewish population. The Greeks had become the new rulers of Egypt as they had conquered most of the lands in the Middle East by defeating the Persians. They allowed the Jews to live autonomously, have their own courts, and take care of themselves. The Greeks trusted the Jews and the Jews respected them for their culture and philosophy, and for the care they displayed for their health and bodies. This was the time when the Greek authorities asked the Jews of Alexandria to produce the Septuagint which was the Bible written by seventy-two Jews (third century B.C.E.). The Septuagint was the original Bible, and was written in Greek.

However, in later years, the Maccabees went to war with the Greeks over their interference at the Temple in Jerusalem.

Philo of Alexandria was a Hellenistic Jew who was born at about 15 B.C.E. He was a philosopher and historian. He protected the memory of Moses who had been disparaged by the Hellenists saying that Moses did not do much on his own. He merely carried out God's orders, performed a few miracles which were really God's miracles, never thought of rescuing the Jews from slavery – only followed God's orders to lead them out of Egypt, and was generally passive while performing only under duress. Philo countered in favor of Moses, saying that he was calm and resolute, and was a great leader. Single-handedly and without a fight he moved an entire nation to a new land - a job that nobody else could have done.

In about 115 C.E. a revolt by the Jews against the Romans started in Libya and spread to Egypt, involving Alexandria. The Romans had become the new conquerors of Mesopotamia, Palestine and North Africa. They had destroyed the Temple in Jerusalem, exiled the Jews from their land and displayed much cruelty. Hatred for Rome, after simmering for a number of years, boiled over in the form of a Jewish revolt whereby many Roman soldiers and guards were killed. The Romans eventually took control of the situation after much loss of life on both sides.

The Muslims spread from Arabia throughout the Middle East in the 7th century C.E. Egypt was conquered by the Arab hordes, and the Jews continued with their own lives uninterrupted, except for the dhimmi – where all non-Muslims had to pay a tax and display humility for not being Muslims. Life was reasonable most of the time in Egypt, except under one Caliph who forced conversions upon the Jews and burnt the dwellings of those who did not respond.

Maimonides, also known as Rambam (initials of his full name, Rabbi Moses Ben Maimon) was born in Cordoba, Spain. He lived from 1135 to 1204. His mother died at an early age. When he was 13, anti-Jewish riots broke out in Cordoba, and his father escaped with the family to Morocco. Five years later, the family moved to Fustat, which is the old city of Cairo. There he studied the Torah, the Mishna, and also became a physician. He later became the physician to Saladin, the ruler of Egypt and Syria. He became famous as a Hebrew and Biblical scholar. He wrote books on religion, medicine and philosophy. Many hospitals are named after him. He wrote the book "Guide for the Perplexed", which is still being read by the intelligentsia of today. He was one of the most famous Jews who ever lived.

Mamelukes were slave-soldiers living in Egypt. They were not native Egyptians, but originally imported from Turkey and Crimea in order to do the hard work in Egypt. In 1250 they revolted and grabbed power, taking over the government in Egypt; they ruled for over 250 years. During their reign, at the time of the Spanish Inquisition, a large stream of Jews came into Egypt in order to escape the Inquisition. In 1517 the Mamelukes were defeated by the Ottomans in the Ottoman-Mameluke War, thus bringing Egypt into the Ottoman Empire.

Muhammad Ali was born in Macedonia into an Albanian family. He led an army that attacked Egypt in a three-way war against the Mamelukes, who were still causing trouble there even though they had been defeated in the past war. He defeated his foes and made himself the commander of Egypt within the Ottoman Empire after receiving Ottoman recognition. He ruled Egypt from about 1805 to 1848 and modernized it. His dynasty continued in Egypt until about 1950. During Muhammad Ali's time Egypt received an injection of Ashkenazi Jews who were escaping from the pogroms in the Pale of Settlement on the Russian border. Until that time all Egyptian Jews had been Sephardim (Spanish Jews) and Mizrahim (Middle Eastern Jews), but these were the first Eastern European Jews (Ashkenazim) to come to Egypt.

Then at the end of the 19th century and beginning of the 20th century Zionism began to spread amongst the Jews all over the world as a result of the encouragement received from Theodor Herzl. Herzl saw no end to anti-Semitism unless the Jews returned to the land of their historical beginnings. Towards the end of the First World War the Balfour Declaration was issued by Britain, wherein it was stated that His Majesty's government views with favor the establishment in Palestine of a national home for the Jews. Jews began to become hopeful, at last, of a future where there would be a Jewish National Home after twenty-five hundred years of wandering. However, coinciding with the Balfour Declaration Britain also promised the Arabs independence for their assistance in fighting against the Ottoman Empire in World War I. Instead, Britain and France shared the Middle East at the end of the war, while Britain slowed down emigration of Jews to Palestine.

At the same time the Wafd Party was developing in Egypt. It fought against the Khedive of Egypt and was later responsible for Egyptian independence from Britain which finally arrived in1922, even though British influence continued, especially because she and France still owned the Suez Canal. In the 1930s Nazism reared its ugly head, and Jews in Egypt worried about the threats being received via the mouth of Adolph Hitler within Germany and spreading into the Middle East, as well as the xenophobia and anti-Semitism coming from the Wafd Party. World War II and the Holocaust followed. At the Wannsee Conference in Germany in 1942 the German leadership decided on the final solution in order to exterminate the Jews. The system of death camps and the use of poison gases were pre-planned. Most of the Jewish population of Europe was annihilated during the world war, leaving a minority of survivors homeless after most of their families were slaughtered.

After World War II the United Nations divided Palestine into two sections – one for the Jews and one for the Palestinians. The Jews accepted the partition plan, but the Palestinians did not. The war between Arab and Jew that followed the Declaration of the Independence of Israel in 1948 led to a Jewish victory, but anti-Jewish riots flared and spread all over Egypt, with destruction of Jewish property and synagogues in Cairo. Arabs were prepared to sacrifice their lives in order to create harm and death to the Jews because of martyrdom in the after-life, as promised to them in the Koran. 80,000 Jews fled Egypt, leaving perhaps a few dozen behind. The infant state of Israel was attacked by its Arab neighbors, led by Egypt, Syria, Iraq and Jordan, but survived the war in which they fought with an untrained and inexperienced army. They possessed one thing, and that was a will to hold on to a two-thousand- year-old dream. It was this dream that won the war and subsequent wars with neighboring Arab states!

In 1956 General Abdul Nasser took over the Suez Canal which was owned by Britain and France (they had been collecting the tolls from the ships that were using the Canal). The Suez Canal was originally built by De Lesseps of France to shorten the sea route to the East from Western Europe, instead of going all the way round the southern tip of Africa. Britain, France and Israel immediately invaded the Suez region after Nasser's takeover. Israel invaded because of the threat to her overseas life-line which was mainly through the Suez Canal, while Britain and France saw it as a theft of their property. General Eisenhower complained that the invasion by Britain, France and Israel had not been discussed with him or the United States, and ordered all three countries to withdraw immediately, which they did. This was a victory for Egypt who gained a major waterway, and for the USSR (Egypt's ally) as this was a skirmish at the time of the Cold War. It also obviously aggravated the Egypt-Israel relationship.

In 1979 Anwar Sadat (who followed Nassar as Egypt's president) and Menachem Begin (prime minister of Israel) signed a Peace Treaty, which, on paper, improved the relationship between the two countries. The Sinai Peninsula, which had been taken by Israel from Egypt during the 1967 war, was returned to Egypt in exchange for peace. This was the first friendship treaty between Israel and an Arab land. However, it was not too popular amongst the mass of Egyptian people who did not wish to have any friendship with Israel. In fact, Sadat was assassinated thereafter because of the signing of the Treaty. Relations between Israel and Egypt are satisfactory at present. Egypt, like Israel, is guarding the Gaza borders and generally co-operating with Israel as far as the Palestinians are concerned. Above all, Egypt and Israel are friends.

JEWS ON THE ARABIAN PENINSULA

By the 6th and 7th centuries there was a rather active Jewish population in Arabia, mostly living in Mecca and Medina. They were business men and dealers who, with their families, frequented the Silk Road. At this time Mohammed was tending to his aunt's camels, and taking them out on their daily trips for feeding purposes. On these daily jaunts he said he met Archangel Gabriel who told him all about Allah and stimulated his interest in monotheism and the worship of Allah. From these visits with Archangel Gabriel, he was able to develop his new religion – Islam. We believe that he really received his information – not from Archangel Gabriel, but from the Jewish residents of Mecca. In fact, he formulated most of his ideas bearing a close relationship to Judaism, even to the smallest details of holy days, rituals and rites. When he invited the Jews to join him in Islam by telling them how close Judaism and Islam were, they refused to do so. He went to war with them, killing them and laying waste to their vineyards. Even today no Jews are permitted to live in Mecca or Medina. Judaism or any other religion is not allowed to be practiced in Saudi Arabia. In the case of Jewish members of the US Military forces stationed on Saudi territory and wishing to pray on the Sabbath or on Jewish holy days, they have to leave Saudi territory and go on to a US warship for the purpose of prayer. The Saudis have madrassahs (religious schools) where many Islamists from Saudi Arabia and other lands are trained to practice a very strict and conservative form of Islam. From these madrassahs a large number of terrorists and soldiers for ISIS have had their training.

Yemen, which has been a home to Jews for thousands of years, is also on the Arabian Peninsula. Jews have been living there since the days of King Solomon, who originally sent them there for the purpose of finding gold and silver for the construction of the Temple.

In the second century of the Common Era a local king living in a portion of Yemen, known as Himyar, converted to Judaism. With him a large number of Yemenis did the same. Hard to believe, but there was a Jewish Kingdom in Yemen for a few hundred years. When news arrived in Yemen concerning the torture and murders of Jews that were being perpetrated in Constantinople by the Byzantine Christians, King Joseph of Himyar, in 523, during a spurt of desire for revenge attacked Christians who were living in his land, killing those who would not convert to Judaism. The Byzantines were distressed to hear about these happenings, but were not willing to go to war as far afield as Yemen. Instead, they arranged with Ethiopian Christians to handle the matter. An Ethiopian army crossed the Red Sea, attacked the Jewish kingdom and replaced it with a Christian kingdom.

The Persians, at this time in history, apart from being opposed to Byzantium, were quite enamored by the Jews. You will remember how King Cyrus of Persia who conquered Babylon after Nebuchadnezzar had exiled the Jews to Babylon, allowed all Jews back to the Holy Land if they wished to return. On this occasion the Persians came and drove the Ethiopians out of Yemen. Most of the Middle East was now in Persian hands.

Jews continued to reside and do business in Yemen until the Arab-Israeli War of 1948. Life was relatively calm and comfortable, as there were few restrictions placed upon them by Yemeni authorities. Following the Arab-Israel War in 1948 life in Yemen became unpredictable. Operation Magic Carpet in 1949 and 1950 saw Israel air-lifting tens of thousands of Jewish citizens of Yemen to Israel. Today almost a half a million Yemenite Jews live in Israel while perhaps a handful of them still reside in Yemen.

JEWS IN IRAN

Firstly, we must remember that Iran is not an Arab land. It is an Islamic country and is in the Middle East. Generally speaking, Iranians have displayed little love towards the Arabs. Much of Iran's history is involved with its neighbors, many of whom are Arabs.

The religion of Persia under Cyrus was Zoroastrian. Zoroastrian is a monotheistic religion, stressing good and evil, and thought by many to be the forerunner of Judaism, which means that it is also the forerunner of Christianity and Islam. After Cyrus conquered Babylon and allowed those

Jews who wished to return to Judea to do so, he also allowed the Jews left in Babylon to practice their own religion. They were pleased with Cyrus. However, in 642 the Muslims conquered Persia and brought Islam to the Persians and to the lands which Persia controlled (including Babylon). This put an end to 12 centuries of Persian domination and Zoroastrianism. Non-Muslim members of the Persian Empire became inferior citizens. Christians and Jews had to wear distinctive badges and were subject to the dhimmi. Zoroastrians who refused conversion to Islam were abused and persecuted, and forced to subscribe to dhimmi laws as promulgated by the Muslims.

In the 13th century Mongol hordes arrived, and the Persian population was decimated, including Muslims and non-Muslims alike. When the Mongols finally departed Muslim control returned via the Ottoman Empire, but this time Persia received a Shiite education. The Shia differ from the vast majority of Muslims who are Sunni. While Mohammed was still alive Ali had been chosen, supposedly by Allah, to succeed him. But when Mohammed died Abu Bakr – and not Ali -became the Caliph. The Shia believe that only Allah can choose a prophet. Therefore, they say that the Muslims erred in replacing Ali (son-in-law and cousin of Mohammed) with Abu Bakr. This has caused a rift between Shia and Sunni which has lasted for the past thirteen hundred years – and, with time, there has been no diminution in the fight between them.

The Shia forced the Jews to abandon their religion and turn to Islam while all synagogues were closed and taken over by the authorities. Many Jews led a double life, pretending that they were Muslims on the outside – they did not have to pay dhimmi nor wear a yellow ribbon, which were pluses; but they were still spiritually and secretly Jews. When they were not observed by the Muslims, at home or amongst their friends, they prayed to the Jewish God and practiced their rituals. Obviously, if they were found out they paid with their lives.

Things changed in the 1660s when Jews were again allowed to practice their own religion. Many of them became merchants and participated in international trade, which was growing at this time. They helped spur the Persian economy. By the 20th century Rezah Shah of the Pahlavi Dynasty permitted equal rights to all religious groups. He put an end to mass conversions and the belief that all non-Muslims were unclean. Hebrew was allowed to be taught in schools and Hebrew newspapers were circulated right until the time that Adolph Hitler appeared on the world stage. Persia changed its name to Iran in 1935. The Allies took control of Iran which had been neutral during World War II in order that that Germany would not be able to get hold of its oil supply.

In 1950 Israel was recognized by Iran as a state. Then in 1979 the Shah was toppled and Iran became an Islamic Republic under the Ayatollah Khomeini. He verbally attacked Israel and Zionism, and ever since then Iran has spoken of destroying Israel, a land that was described by Khomeini as a filthy nation. They respect the fact that Jews are monotheists, and they allow Jews to run for government positions in their elections. They say that they have nothing against Jews per se; their argument is with Israel. Jews have been living fairly well in Iran, but there have been cases of trials against Jews who have been accused of being agents of Israel, and the law weighs heavily against them. The population of Jews in Iran is down from about 80,000 to less than 30,000 – the largest concentration of Jews in the Middle East outside Israel.

JEWS IN SYRIA

We are told that in the days after the death of Jesus Paul of Tarsus converted Jews to Christianity in Damascus. At this time Jews were also known to be living in Aleppo. By 635 the Muslims arrived, and Syria turned toward Islam. Damascus became the capital of the Umayyad Dynasty. In the 12th century the Crusaders conquered the Holy Land and placed heavy taxation on the Jews. If the Jews were not paying taxes to the Muslims for being Jews, they were now paying taxes to the Christians for not being Christian. Therefore, many Jews from the Holy Land, in order to escape taxation, fled to Damascus, where, I am sure, they had to pay taxes to the Muslims again. When Saladin retrieved the Holy Land from the Crusaders, and most of the Middle East came under his control, conditions improved for the Jews. Jews had fought under Saladin against the Crusaders. However, after the death of Saladin the situation reverted.

The Spanish Inquisition of 1492 brought Sephardic Jews, who did not wish to convert to Islam, to Syria where the situation was not good, but certainly better than death by the Inquisition.

The Damascus Affair took place in 1840. It was a case of ritual murder committed by Druzes and Muslims upon a Christian, Father Thomas. Jews were blamed for the murders, and 63 Jewish children were kidnapped so as to perhaps make their parents confess. Other Jews were arrested and tortured, forcing a false confession by some of them. Sir Moses Montefiore of England and other European experts were called in by the Jews of Damascus in order to assist in establishing fair play. The final outcome saved the lives of the suspected Jews that were still alive; three had died as a result of torture and burning.

Under the French mandate following World War I Jews had a difficult time in Syria. There were anti-Jewish riots, and subsequently immigration of Jews to France, Palestine and elsewhere. In 1946 Syria received independence from France. Attempts at a Jewish escape from Syria was prevented by the new Alawite administration, but somehow many Jews got away, either to Turkey or Lebanon. The Alawites are an off-shoot from Shia Muslims, but are not recognized by Muslims as being a part of their faith because they also have a mixture of many Christian rituals and beliefs. Belief in the Trinity is regarded by some Muslims as polytheism because one is praying to God, Jesus and Mother Mary, and perhaps to some Saints, as well.

THE MAGHREB

The Jews have been living in the Maghreb ever since the time of King Solomon. The Maghreb is the northern part of Africa including the Atlas Mountains, Morocco, Algeria, Tunisia and Libya. They had been traveling in their boats with the Phoenicians, and trading with the local populations. They settled amongst the Berbers, and some Berbers converted to Judaism. I daresay some Jews might have become Berber. There were further infusions of Jews over the centuries into the Maghreb following the Roman conquest of Palestine in 70 C.E., the failed Jewish revolt under Bar Kochba in 138 C.E., the Spanish and Portuguese Inquisitions from 1492 and thereafter, and as a result of pogroms in Eastern Europe in the 19th century and when Fascism arrived in Mussolini's Italy and Hitler's Third Reich.

They had their ups and downs living under Muslim domination. One bright feature of Jewish history in the Maghreb was in Morocco under

King Mohammed V during the second World War. In 1940 France was invaded by the Nazis. The Vichy government (which was the French government in control of France's overseas possessions and naval forces) was allowed by Germany to control the French Empire as Hitler had no time for "small" matters while he was busy fighting for world domination. The Germans called via the Vichy government for King Mohammed of Morocco (Morocco was a French possession) to restrict the Jews and to send many to Germany for the gas chambers. King Mohammed refused to do so. He said "the Jews of Morocco are our people, and we will treat them like the rest of our people".

Jews have been living in Libya since Biblical days. King Solomon traded with surrounding lands and North Africa. Jews continued living there through the Greek and Roman periods. Their populations were boosted at the time of the Spanish Inquisition. They lived under the rule of the Muslim leadership and the Italian take-over at the beginning of the twentieth century. By the late 1930s under Mussolini matters deteriorated, especially after Mussolini became influenced by Hitler, his Axis partner. Jews were sent to concentration camps amidst many pogrom-like episodes. After World War II and the leadership of Qaddafi, living conditions continued to deteriorate. The creation of the State of Israel merely added fuel to the fire, and anti-Jewish riots became worse. Many Libyan Jews have immigrated to Israel as well as Italy. Today there are no Jews in Libya.

There have been Jews living in Algeria since the early years of the Common Era, as in other parts of North Africa. France occupied Algeria in 1830. Thereafter more Jews arrived, adopting the French culture, and in 1870 they were offered French citizenship. Towards the beginning of World War II, they were attacked by Muslims in Algeria, having been influenced by events in Germany. After Germany conquered France in World War II Algerian Jews were persecuted by the Vichy government. Vichy withdrew citizenship rights from the Jews. The only action left to Algerian Jews was to participate in the Free French resistance movement, which they did. The Free French movement was a thorn in the side of the Axis powers. Finally, the American forces arrived and liberated Algeria from Vichy control.

In 1962 Algeria received independence from France. Jews in the country were harassed and their economic rights were interfered with.

130,000 Jews left for France, Israel and the United States. Synagogues became mosques and the lives of Jews in Algeria became only a memory. In 2018 Algerian Jews and those who had lived in Algeria before being forced out were compensated by the German government as part of the Holocaust compensation which they were paying out to European Jewish victims.

Jews also departed from neighboring Tunisia where they similarly had a long history. Tunisian Jews started to move out following an anti-Zionist and anti-Israel reaction in 1948 when Israel was declared a state.

JEWS IN TURKEY

Turkey is not considered to be a part of the Middle East. It is mostly in Asia Minor with a portion of Istanbul in Europe, but the Ottoman Empire ruled over the Middle East from the 16th to the 20th Century. It is also a Muslim country, and is thus no Middle Eastern stranger.

The first Jew to arrive in Turkey was Noah who came in his Ark, with two of every species of creatures of this world on board. He traveled through the Flood in his Ark and made landfall at Ararat in the eastern portion of the Taurus mountains in Anatolia, Turkey. Apparently, he did not stay there for very long, and we do not hear about Turkey for many centuries after that.

The Roman Empire extended into Anatolia, and later a large portion of it became the Byzantine Empire, which was the eastern part of the Roman Empire. Jews had followed the Romans into their Empire after they were expelled from Jerusalem in 70 C.E. and after the Bar Kochba Revolt in 138 C.E. Thus, many of them became residents of Constantinople.

In 1204 the Crusaders attacked and laid waste to Constantinople, which demonstrates the enmity between the Christians of Western Europe and those of Eastern Europe, which was the Byzantine Empire. Mehmet drove the Byzantines out of Constantinople in 1453, and made it the capital of Islam. By this time Damascus and Baghdad were fading. He immediately went to the Hagia Sophia Church which had been built by the Byzantines – the largest church in the world – and converted it into a mosque. Today it is a museum.

In 1492 the Sultan of Turkey invited the Jews from Spain when they were expelled during the Spanish Inquisition – also following the

Portuguese Inquisition – to come and live in Turkey. They were invited because of their legendary ability in business, and to improve the economy of Turkey. Since the days of Mehmet, the Jews were already becoming involved in the finances of Constantinople and playing a large role in the cultural and political life. Mehmet concentrated Anatolian Jews and Christians into Constantinople for re-building a damaged city – damaged by wars and by the Crusader attacks in the past, as well as the Black Death of 1347. This, despite the fact that Jews and Christians were second class citizens, having to pay the dhimmi and requiring to remain humble and not be conspicuous.

Most Jews in Turkey were Sephardim (over 90%), but Ashkenazim were becoming more prominent, as a famous rabbi had encouraged them to come to Anatolia because (he said) "Isn't it better to live under the Muslims than to live with the Christians?"

One Jewish woman who came to Turkey at the invitation of the Sultan of Turkey following the Spanish, and later, the Portuguese Inquisitions was Gracia Mendes. She was a family member of a wealthy Jewish family, first from Spain and later, Portugal. She developed a large business emporium which had been started by her deceased husband, doing business with most of Europe. She arrived in Constantinople, and donated large sums of money to Jewish causes throughout the known world. She published numerous valuable Hebrew texts before, as she believed, they would disappear from the world. She was a Zionist before Herzl. She asked the Sultan of Turkey if he would allow an expedition to Tiberias, led by her son-in-law to establish a home for the Jews in Tiberias, which would remain as a part of the Ottoman Empire. The Sultan gave permission. The expedition went to Tiberias, struggled along for some months, but failed. Conditions were unbearable, disease was rampant, people died in large numbers from infections. Preparations were inadequate, and the survivors returned to Constantinople.

Sabbatai Zvi was a Sephardic rabbi born in Smyrna (now Izmir) in 1626. He claimed to be the Messiah. His claim appeared to be very strong and was recognized by the most prominent Jews in Turkey, and after a while, in the rest of the world. Many rabbis assured their congregations that he was the true Messiah. Non-Jewish Holy men also believed that he might be the Messiah, including Muslims. At this stage many people throughout the world had been suffering a great deal and had been praying for a Messiah. In fact, the Muslim authorities did not interfere with Sabbatai's claim since they thought that perhaps he was the true Messiah, as they had been anticipating the arrival of the Mahdi. He seemed to be the right man at the right time. People did not wish to deny his claims because if he turned out to be the real Messiah they might be punished. Some Jews throughout the world had removed a portion of the wall or roof of their homes so that they would somehow receive early messaging of the arrival of the Messiah. However, only when Sabbatai announced 'we are all going to Jerusalem, so don't pay your taxes to the Sultan', did the Sultan have him arrested. He was given the alternative of either converting to Islam or face death. He chose Islam! Jews could not believe it. The Holiest of Holies turned away from the Jewish God! Subsequently he lived as a Muslim, but was frequently seen saying his Hebrew prayers. The False Messiah died as a Muslim.

However, there were many followers of the False Messiah, despite his conversion to Islam. They said he was a very smart man, and he probably converted, only for the purpose of bringing the Jews and Islam closer together. Even some Muslims joined them, agreeing that there must have been a reason for his conversion. They are known as the 'donmeh', and they consist of Jews and Muslims. They have formed schools in Thessaloniki and Istanbul where they follow the teachings of Sabbatai Zvi. With time they have developed into more of a Muslim association. They marry only within their own group, and tend to be secretive about their private lives. They seem to have become more Muslim than Jewish. Out of them have come the Young Turks who were responsible for the removal of the Turkish Caliphate and possibly the decimation of the Armenians in Turkey. The Young Turks consisted mostly of Turks, but also Jews, Greeks, Arabs and Albanians. Kemal Ataturk, who had also belonged to the Young Turks and was educated in a 'donmeh' school, was the founder of Modern Turkey.

Ataturk separated religion from government while he was the first President of Turkey. He altered Turkey's course away from theocracy, separating government from religion. He Westernized Turkey, changed the alphabet to a Western style, and got rid of the fez. He was respectful towards the Jews. In the 1920s he arranged a population exchange with Greece whereby Turkish citizens in Greece were returned to Turkey and

Greeks in Turkey were returned to Greece. This brought thousands of Jews to Turkey, including many members of the 'donmeh' thus saving these thousands of Jews from the Nazi death camps when Hitler ordered the Greek Jews to be brought to his prison camps during the Holocaust. He was also responsible for allowing safe passage for Jews fleeing from the Nazis in the 1930s.

At the start of the 20th century there were 200,000 Jews living in Turkey. In 1942 the Turkish government created a wealth tax. Jews were hit very hard by this tax. They felt that it was an anti-Semitic gesture that was created to get as many as possible to leave the country. Ataturk, at this stage, had died. Also, at this time the Second World War was taking place and even though Turkey was neutral the government responded to the demands of the Nazis to send as many Jews as possible to their internment camps and ultimately as fodder for their gas chambers. All this time there was a trickle of Jews leaving Turkey for Palestine and some for the United States.

The Struma was a ship coming from Romania with 780 Jews aboard escaping from the death camps of Europe and hoping to arrive in Palestine, but the British would not allow them to go there even though the Balfour Declaration viewed in favor of the Jews having a national home in Palestine. The Struma wandered the Black Sea seeking a place that would accept them as refugees. The ship was in poor condition, but, arriving in Istanbul, they were not allowed to dock. They were towed away, and 780 Jews went down with the Struma, the largest civilian sea disaster of World War II.

Today there are probably about 13,000 Jews in Turkey. The present President, Erdogan, is no friend of the Jews, especially since the 2010 Gaza Flotilla, which Erdogan sent to break the boycott of Gaza set up by Israel as a result of the problems they were having with Hamas and the Gaza residents. Israel sent her navy in to prevent Erdogan's flotilla from breaking the blockade and arriving at Gaza. Erdogan appears to be eroding all the advances that were introduced by Kemal Ataturk. Also, the wonderful gesture of the Sultan of Turkey who invited the Jews to come to Turkey after the Inquisition in 1492 has now been neutralized by the latest actions of the present-day President of Turkey.

ISRAEL

Israel is not an Arab land, but a Jewish land which was created by the United Nations after World War II. It is surrounded by numerous Arab lands which, went to war with this embryonic country in order to prevent its birth and very existence. We have been discussing the diaspora of Jews, originally from their Biblical Homeland, becoming refugees in Arab lands throughout the Ages, but there has always been a yearning, a prayer, by the Jews to return to the land of their ancestors – a diaspora in reverse, an aching desire to return to the womb! Do we not cry out in the synagogues "Next year in Jerusalem"?

After World War II the survivors of the Holocaust required a home. For those who did not have relatives in the Free World there was no place to turn, but to Israel. Since the end of the nineteenth century Theodore Herzl and the Zionist Movement had declared that it was necessary for the Jews to have a national home in the land of their Biblical roots. Zionism grew amongst the Jewish population world-wide. Jews were beginning to return to Zion, but Britain who had the mandate over Palestine set up barriers preventing their return. This was strange as the Balfour Declaration, signed by Lord Balfour for the British government, declared that Britain viewed with favor, a home for the Jews in Palestine. Of course, simultaneously Britain had also made similar promises to the Middle Eastern Arabs, and was trying to maintain the peace in the days when the Jews were trying to escape the Holocaust in order to survive. Many thousands of desperate and needy Jews were prevented from entering the Holy Land. In 1948 the General Assembly of the United Nations voted to divide Palestine in two – a land for the Arabs and one for the Jews.

After a number of Israel-Arab wars, outnumbered by perhaps twenty to one, fighting with a make-shift and untrained army – but with a will which told them that a loss of one battle would probably mean a loss of the land forever – the Israelis succeeded in all the wars. In fact, they actually occupied territory from which the Arabs were forced to retreat. Jews entered Israel from all corners of the world to help fight for their existence. People who were secular Jews and had never thought seriously about Israel or religion suddenly woke up and became patriots, wanting to go Home. Survivors of the Holocaust, Jews from Arab lands, Black Jews from Africa, Asian Jews from India and China, all returned to Israel. Some Catholics from South America whose ancestors were Jews and were forced by the Spanish and Portuguese Inquisitions to convert to Catholicism now converted back to Judaism and went to live in Israel. Many Jews who had been happy in their own countries in the United States, the British Empire, Russia and Europe also came to Israel for patriotic or religious reasons.

The love-hate relationship between Jews and Arabs has continued until this day. The Jews have been living in Arab lands continuously for 2500 years. In fact, they preceded Islam by about fifteen hundred years. The world congress of nations – the United Nations – declared a small area of the Middle East, perhaps 2%, as a home for the Jews who had suffered almost three millennia of torture and destruction. This little slab of land given to them was sufficient cause for the neighboring Arab countries to attack the infant state of Israel and attempt to put an end to its existence, even though it had scarcely taken a breath. Their attempt failed, and they failed again repeatedly after subsequent wars and intifadas. They have stated over and over again that they would not be satisfied until the last Jew was driven out of Arab lands.

Palestine has never been governed by the Palestinians. In Biblical days the land was the home of the Canaanites, the Philistines and Phoenicians. When the Jews returned from Egypt after their forty-year sojourn in the desert they conquered the land and lived there, first under Judges, then under Kings. After that, the land was split into two Jewish Kingdoms, Judea and Israel. Israel was later conquered by the Assyrians and Judea was taken over by the Babylonians. The Persians conquered the Babylonians. Then Alexander the Great, a Macedonian, took control of the Holy Land from the Persians. Alexander's territory was turned over to the Greeks, the greatest and most advanced nation at that time. The Greeks were defeated by the Romans who called the land Palestine. Islam arrived in the seventh century, calling out "Allah or the sword", and dominated the entire Middle East and North Africa. The Mongols then invaded parts of the Middle East, but could not sustain their Empire. The Ottomans (also an Islamic people) first defeated and drove out the Byzantines from Asia Minor, before conquering South-eastern Europe, the Middle East and North Africa where they ruled until the end of World War I. Palestine, together with the rest of the Middle East, then fell under Ottoman rule. The British and French took over most of the Middle East and North Africa after the Treaty of Versailles. At about this time the Ottoman Empire came to an end, and following the end of World War I Britain and France ruled the Middle East, including Palestine by mandate from the League of Nations. Palestine fell under the British. After World War II most of the Arab lands became independent, but Palestine still remained under the British mandate. In 1948 the United Nations divided Palestine into two sections – one for the Jews and one for the Palestinians, who rejected the division because they did not want any division – they wanted it all. The West Bank which was the part of Palestine outside the Israeli sector, was given to Jordan, as the Palestinians did not accept the partition of the land.

The Palestinians say that the Jews have grabbed their country; not so, it was given to them by the world body – the United Nations (if Biblical history is not enough to prove anything). So, when was Palestine ever in Palestinian hands? Never, as you can see from the list of rulers enumerated above, from the Canaanites to the British, and finally, Israel. Apart from the wars fought on behalf of the Palestinians by their Arab brothers, the Palestinians have created a number of intifadas (insurrections, an Arab word meaning 'shaking off') against Israel, with the killing of some Israelis. Rockets have been aimed at Israeli targets all over the country, and, generally speaking, the Palestinian sector has been responsible for much terrorism.

There have been demands from many parts of the world calling for sanctions against Israel for its handling of the Palestinians with a heavy hand, but how else would other countries have treated a hostile band who had sworn never to give in until the last Jew had left their land? Rockets consistently land on Israel soil, occasionally causing property damage and the loss of life. They don't want peace; they don't want a One-State or a Two-State Solution. They just want Israel to get off the land which they have never owned! The United Nations, the United States and some Arab countries have supplied the Palestinians with financial aid. This makes it less urgent for them to make a decision for a One State or Two-State solution, while most of them are living in refugee camps in other Arab lands. Nor have they been granted citizenship or a vote in those lands, whereas the Palestinians living in Israel have both citizenship and a vote.

At present there appears to be a re-alignment of friend and foe in the

Middle East. Until now, all the Arab nations have been on the same side as far as the Palestinian problem is concerned, and Israel has been the enemy. Things are changing. Ever since the United Nations divided Palestine in two in order to accommodate Israel and the Palestinians, the Palestinians seem to be content to continue living as refugees and not accepting a two-state solution. The Arab allies are beginning to lose patience. There is another problem. Iran seems to be intent on developing a nuclear bomb. Most of the Arab states are afraid of Iranian aggression, their desire to become the major Muslim state and wishing to spread the Shia creed. Israel has the most powerful army in the neighborhood, and has on a few occasions attacked the Iranian nuclear program and destroyed much of its development through cyber technology. Arab countries are looking to their past enemy to help them against the menace from Iran. Egypt and Jordan already have made peace treaties with Israel. Saudi Arabia has looked the other way when Israel has expanded into the West Bank. Even though the Saudis have not actively sought friendship from Israel, they have said nothing against them and have permitted Israeli planes to fly over their territory. Bahrain and the Emirates are trading with Israel, as is Sudan. All this, to the chagrin of the Palestinians! Israel, the enemy of yesterday, may yet become the ally of tomorrow!

NEEDLESS WARS

*F*or a country that loves peace, America has been involved in 93 wars since it fought for its independence in 1776, which was almost 250 years ago. This includes small wars and large wars, necessary wars and wars that many believe were unnecessary. These wars have been fought at a tremendous cost in lives, dollars, broken hearts and broken homes, and chronic physical and psychological complications inflicted upon the survivors. Some of the wars were essential as they were fought for freedom and democracy, or for saving innocent populations from the hands of tyrants, despots and mad men. I, however, will concentrate on those wars that might not have been quite as necessary, those in which the losses outweighed the benefits. There is also a question of wars, especially against Native Americans which many will consider to be immoral.

WAR OF 1812

We hear very little of the War of 1812. It came soon after the American Revolution when the new United States declared war on Britain. Still in its infancy, this new self-governing land had the audacity to declare war on one of the most powerful nations on earth, a nation with the largest navy and a rapidly expanding empire. Was it a brave move or a rather thoughtless move? It almost sounds self-destructive. Yet the 1812 war continued for over two years, and even though it was declared a draw by historians the American republic achieved some of the goals for which it went to war, but also suffered many disappointments.

The new free land had been prospering rather well after the War of Independence. You might say "Don't worry about small annoyances. Rather go ahead and build up your country". Britain, at that time was at war with France, fighting in the Napoleonic battles in Europe. British ships were sailing the Atlantic, both for trade and for war maneuvers. The British navy was stopping US ships, boarding them, and grabbing American sailors for service on British ships. This was known as impressment. It was totally disrespectful, as well as a crime at sea, akin to piracy. At the same time the British had been interfering in the US trade with France by blockading American ports. France had assisted the American colonies in their war with England. On land, the British had been aiding Native Americans who were attacking American citizens on the Canadian border. Native Americans had been unhappy that the American colonists had won independence from Britain. They felt that they had been mistreated by Americans in the past and feared for their future. The British, however, were still continuing to help Native Americans with their problems at the hands of the Americans.

Covertly, the new United States felt that they might be able to invade Canada, conquer it, and make it a part of the new United States. Many were convinced that this would not be difficult, especially as the British home base was thousands of miles away on the other side of the Atlantic - one of the reasons that they lost the War of Independence. Blockade of American shipping and impressment of American sailors into the British navy could be considered good reasons for going to war, but invasion of Canada for the purpose of conquering a country in order to extend one's territory is, perhaps, less ethical.

The United States declared war on Great Britain in 1812. James Madison was President at the time. The declaration was ratified by Congress. The first part of the war was fought in Canada, a British colony. Americans invaded Canada. They were inadequately trained, and did not make any real progress. Much of the fighting took place on the Great Lakes, especially Erie and Ontario, where the British had built forts which were well manned. William Harrison, who later became President, defeated Tecumseh, a Native Chief, at Thames, Ontario. Tecumseh had been organizing tribesmen in order to set up a Native American Confederacy.

Native American tribes fought on the side of Britain, as did escaped slaves from the southern states. The only African-Americans fighting with the US forces were those (a small number) on ships, as the Army would not accept them in its forces.

There was much argument amongst Americans about the war. The northern industrial part of the United States was not in favor of the war, as they knew that the British were far ahead in the Industrial Revolution, and they were in favor of their own industrial development as well, and did not want to delay any advances. The southern farmers and planters were pro-war because they disliked the British who were still fighting against France at the same time. They did not care about the Industrial Revolution. They were also pro-France, and they hoped for a French victory against Britain.

There was more fighting in the United States itself. The British attacked Baltimore. Frances Scott Keys witnessed the battle at Fort MacHenry, which influenced him to write the words to The Star- Spangled Banner. Washington was attacked and burned, and the White House, too, was burned down. Andrew Jackson, who later became president, was the hero who took New Orleans from the British. This battle took place after the war was over. The Treaty of Ghent had already been signed on Christmas Day, 1814, but news traveled slowly in pre-telegraph and pre-telephone days. The news of the Peace Treaty had not arrived yet when in January 1815 Jackson with the help of the famous pirate, Jean Lafitte, worked their way through the bayous of Louisiana, and defeated the British. Lafitte had about a thousand men working for him, and at one time had more ships than the US Navy. He was of French extraction, and assisted Jackson in the taking of New Orleans because neither he nor the French wanted to see Louisiana under British control since it was the largest port in North America.

After the war America had free control of the seas and there was an economic boom in the country. There was no more impressment. Some have called the 1812 War the Second War of Independence because it clarified some of the borders. It left the Native Americans without aid from the British, and that put an end to their hopes of a future confederacy. There were, however, many more wars with them. Canada thought that she had won the war because she had not been occupied by the American forces. Canada remained within the British Empire, but today it is totally free and self-governing, even though it is a member of the British Commonwealth.

INDIAN WARS

American – Native-American Wars have continued since the time the first colony of settlement opened up in Jamestown. They almost always resulted from arguments concerning land control. The White settlers needed more land and the Natives were in their way. This continued on and off until 1924. Today there are about 6.7 million people who can claim as being descendants of Native Americans. This is about 2% of their original population when the White man arrived. They have succumbed to wars, land grabbing, and infectious diseases such as smallpox and measles against which they had zero immunity. They were also chased out of their lands and sent westward, which required long marches with many dying on the way to their new abodes. Franciscan friars and other religious missionaries came from Europe and converted many to Christianity, driving them away from their families and their centuries-old beliefs.

When the White man arrived and displaced them, wreaking havoc upon their existence they deteriorated as a people, much like the post-traumatic stress disorder described in today's medical journals as occurring in occupied and defeated populations. They had led peaceful agrarian lives while moving around the land until they were forced to change their life-styles.

Their origin is not altogether clear, but there were large migrations from Asia, passing through the Bering Straits about 20,000 years ago. Apparently, in those days the Bering Straits consisted of dry land. It is unlikely, that such a huge continent spanning both hemispheres would only have one entrance into it - up in the far north. There must have been other entrances in other parts of the American continent. There seems to be evidence of Chinese, Filipino and South Sea Islanders of having sailed to the Americas. There is even talk (probably a fable) of the Ten Lost Tribes of Israel having come to the New World.

The First American settlement by Europeans took place in 1607 in Jamestown. The new settlers wanted to own the land whereas the natives felt that the land belonged to nobody, but everybody should be allowed to live on it and not own it. Life was very precarious. Cold, hunger and hardships followed for the people who came from England and hoped to commence a new life. In 1609 the Jamestown Massacre occurred when the Powhatan Indians came down, killing a large number of settlers. The remaining colonists were about to leave when some new settlers arrived, and helped them to start a new life. They brought with them tobacco growing plants.

The Pequot War of 1636 occurred mostly in Massachusetts. It was basically a trade war. The Pequot Indians and some Dutch settlers were trapping animals for their furs and then selling the furs. The Puritans were jealous and wished to improve their own fur trade. In one day about five hundred Pequots were slaughtered. This action, together with a small pox epidemic almost put an end to the Pequot tribe, leaving a mere few hundred behind. This brutal war actually improved the safety of the colonists.

In 1614 New Netherlands was founded and became the first colony of the Netherlands on the American continent with New Amsterdam as its main port. The area was chosen because it promised farmland and a fur trade. The Dutch treated the Indians well. Unfortunately, their colony was badly situated from the Dutch point of view because it acted as a wedge between the British territories of New England and the development around Jamestown to the south. King Charles decided that his brother the Duke of York should invade the New Netherlands. The Dutch left without a fight, many of them returning to Europe. New Amsterdam became New York in 1674. This wedge now filled in the empty space between the British colonies to the north and to the south. Yet the Dutch were satisfied as they received Suriname in South America as an exchange. They thought that Suriname might turn out to be the better part of the bargain – better than New York!

Then there were the Beaver Wars which continued for most of the 17th century. They occurred along the lands bordering on the St. Lawrence River and the Great Lakes. They were fought between the Iroquois and the Algonquins together with their French Allies. This was fought mostly for dominance in the fur trade. France had been the most important power in the fur trade, but by the end of the wars with England she had lost a great deal of her punch, allowing England to take over. The Beaver Wars progressed into, what was known as the Mourning Wars. Native Americans had lost a great many of their young men in these wars which caused much mourning at this time. They fought back against their enemies, killing only a few, but preserving the rest of their men, whom they took home and nurtured in order that they should replace those that they had lost in the fighting. The American colonists were minimally involved in the Beaver Wars.

One of the bloodiest wars involving Native Americans was the Tuscarora War of 1711 where the Tuscarora tribe attacked European settlements in North Carolina. A large number of people were killed on both sides. As a peace settlement after the fighting the Tuscarora Indians consented to live in an area in North Carolina which was set aside for them.

During the American Revolution the Native Americans had sided with Britain, but by the time the revolution was over they had lost a great deal of land to the White Americans, and the land that Britain had protected for them, too, was taken by the Americans. Since they had not been invited to the peace talks, the Native Americans had no say in the matter. They were the original inhabitants of the continent. The land was being removed from under their eyes, but they were never consulted about their own future.

In 1830 President Andrew Jackson brought into effect the Indian Removal Act which ordered all Indians to leave the areas where they were residing and move to the west of the Mississippi River. This sent them scampering long distances – many by foot! Three thousand died as a result of this forced march, called the Trail of Tears.

Andrew Jackson was also involved in the First Seminole War when he was asked by President Monroe to invade Florida in 1818. Florida was a home to escaped slaves, Indians that were constantly interfering with the lives of Southerners living close to the southern borders, and criminals. Jackson attacked, and quietened some of the problems. Florida had been in the hands of Spain for about three hundred years, but in 1821 Spain ceded Florida to the United States. In the 1830s and 1850s there were the Second and Third Seminole Wars whereby the Federal government sent in troops to further control the Seminoles. Their numbers had dwindled down to about three hundred, but now they are in six different reserves in Florida, where they have multiplied.

The Black Hawk war started in 1832 when Chief Black Hawk crossed the border into Illinois to take back the territory that the United States had taken over in an 1804 treaty. Black Hawk had a reputation of having carried out a number of successful skirmishes in the past, but this time he was clearly and easily defeated. It was a one-sided battle, and it also put an end to the disturbances caused by Indians in the Chicago area.

In less than a day in June, 1876 the Sioux tribe and the Cheyenne defeated the U.S. army at Little Bighorn. This was Custer's Last Stand. He was killed, and every man fighting on the U.S. side was killed with him. The Native Americans were led by Crazy Horse and Sitting Bull. When the battle was over, the Cheyenne and the Sioux disappeared for fear of the U.S, returning with a fresh army which would arrive and exact revenge. The Native Americans spread out into small groups for maneuverability, while some of them went farming in Montana. This Battle in which the Americans were severely defeated actually put an end to the Indian wars because the remaining tribes were forced to give up their lands and move into reservations.

The Ghost Dance was a method whereby the Lakota Indians would display their resistance to U.S. policy towards the Indians. In December 1890 at Wounded Knee in South Dakota the Lakota Indians were performing this Dance. The U.S. army attacked them and the spectators during the performance, and killed at least 150 people. This was not a war, but a Massacre. It appears as though the general public did not complain about the cold-blooded killing. As recently as March, 1970 Wounded Knee was re-occupied by the Oglala Lakota Indians for seventy days. There were shootings and some deaths during the occupation. They were complaining about inadequate assistance from the Federal government and poor conditions where they lived, but they also were demonstrating against some of their own internal problems.

There does not appear to be any more wars with the Native Americans, either now or in the future, as they are too weak, decentralized and living in reservations.

MEXICAN WAR

Texas had been a part of Mexico, and many Americans had came to live and farm there because Mexico had invited them to add to the sparse population and also to act as a buffer against the Native Americans. Many Americans responded to the invitation, and had a good life farming in Texas. They felt so much at home that after some time they decided to fight for their independence from Mexico. In 1836 they were defeated by Santa Anna and his Mexican troops at the Siege of Alamo, but Sam Houston and his men followed up on their loss and overcame the Alamo defeat a by a victory over Santa Anna at San Jacinto, gaining independence for Texas from Mexico.

Mexico did not really accept the fact that Texas was free. Nor did Mexico agree with the fact that Texans claimed the Rio Grande as their border. Mexico said that the border was farther north, and sent troops to Texas to confirm this opinion. At this time Texas was calling for American intervention. Thereupon James Polk, the President, asked Congress to declare war upon Mexico. He believed in Manifest Destiny – America was to expand throughout North America so as to improve the lives of all the people living in North America. The U.S. responded by invading Texas. At the same time, they occupied Santa Fe in New Mexico, marched into California and finally entered into Mexico City as a bargaining chip. The war started in1846, and in 1848 the Treaty of Guadalupe Hidalgo was signed. The U.S. gained Texas, much of New Mexico, a large part of Arizona, Colorado, California and a portion of Wyoming. She also paid about 15 million dollars for damages caused. That was a great deal of territory gained as a result of a petty border squabble!

Some have said that this was a righteous war –Texans and Americans were attacked in Texas, and this should not go unpunished. On the other hand, the loss to the United States by Mexico of more than half of their country seems to be a bitter pill to swallow. A border skirmish, and – Boom – there goes the major portion of your country!

The original colony in Jamestown, Virginia, and the Pilgrim colony in Massachusetts had grown tremendously following the Louisiana Purchase and western expansion, and now the Treaty of Guadalupe Hidalgo! The tiny seeds that were planted in the North-East had grown into an over-sized forest!

OVERSEAS WARS

George Washington had warned to stay out of foreign wars and keep aloof from foreign entanglements. This was excellent advice, but I doubt if he would have advised America to stay out of World Wars I and II. It was certainly necessary to enter the conflict in World War I, especially after Germany had tried to get Mexico to attack the United States, and later in World War II, to protect freedom and democracy from a crazy dictator who wanted to control the earth. However, subsequently the U.S. became involved in Asian conflicts which were expensive and caused the loss of a great many lives. These wars caused many more problems than were solved. But first, we will discuss the Spanish-American War.

SPANISH-AMERICAN WAR

Before 1898 Cuba and the Philippines had been clamoring for independence from Spain for some time. Cuba was dissatisfied with the high taxes it paid, lack of political representation, and corrupt and poor administration from Spain. America found herself in a position supporting their moves toward independence. The U.S. wanted to protect American business interests in Cuba and the Philippines while she also had desires for annexation as she wanted European countries out of the American continent despite the fact that Spain did most of the exploration in the Americas. If it was not for Spain and Portugal there might not have been an America! It was a follow-up of the Monroe Doctrine in the early nineteenth century. Cuba, of course, was an island off the American continent, and less than a hundred miles from Florida. Also, the American people seemed to support the anti-Spanish rhetoric of the Cuban government.

A mysterious explosion on the USS Maine which was anchored in Havana harbor brought a declaration of war from the United States against Spain. It turns out that the fire on the Maine was not caused by the Spanish, but was due to a fire in the ship's galley. Yet the war continued without any confirmation of the cause of the fire. However, when the war was over Spain ceded Cuba, the Philippines, Guam and Puerto Rico to the United States. Spain believed that the war was not justified and that the U.S. should have kept her nose out of Spain's private affairs in her own colonies. They said that America's actions were not based on true facts. Anyhow, this war ended Spain's history as a colonial power in the Western Hemisphere. At the same time, it introduced the United States as a Pacific power. It was also the first war in which the U.S. fought outside the United States for the gain of territory in other parts of the world. Prior to this war the U.S. fought for independence, against slavery and for the extension of adjacent land.

KOREAN WAR

The Korean War was a part of the Cold War. Most smaller wars at this time were supported either by the Western Powers or the Soviets as a part of the larger Cold War struggle. Korea had been occupied and was controlled by Japan ever since 1910. However, when Japan surrendered to the Allies in 1945 at the end of World War II the Korean Peninsula was taken out of her hands. No clear decision was decided upon as to the type of government for the future of Korea. The Soviets finally settled for a Communist regime for North Korea while the U.S. and the U.K. pressed for a democratic government for South Korea. In 1948 North Korea formed the People's Army, mostly from the guerillas who had fought with the Chinese Communists in their fight for independence against Chiang Kai-Shek. Soviet advisers assisted the North Koreans in fighting the war against South Korea.

In June 1950 North Korea invaded South Korea. The United Nations immediately supported South Korea. General MacArthur with his military forces landed at Inchon, South Korea and worked their way northwards, driving the North Koreans all the way back to the Yalu River which separated China from North Korea. At this point, China came down to assist the North Koreans, sending the United Nations forces (held together by the Americans) back into South Korea. An armistice was signed, but there was no agreement and no peace treaty. The two Koreas have remained until this day as two separate nations, both still fuming hatred at each other. As a matter of fact, war games are continually on display, especially with North Korea frequently testing new missiles and South Korea repeatedly practicing war maneuvers with her American allies.

This was not considered to be an unnecessary war as much as a failed ending to the war. Nations were tired of war coming so soon after World War II. After the war was fought North and South Korea were still separate nations, officially still at war. Forty thousand American lives were lost while far more Koreans were killed, maimed or became refugees. With the hostility shown towards each other a world-wide conflagration could occur at any time in Korea. Constant threats and warnings have kept both the Communist and Western worlds on edge. We should have worked harder for a Korean peace.

VIETNAM WAR

Japanese control of Vietnam existed during World War II, but when Japan was forced to give up its Empire at the end of the war Vietnam found itself in the hands of France once again, as Vietnam had been part of French-Indo China before the war. In 1954 France, following the battle at Dien Bien Phu, was forcibly ejected from Vietnam. At the conference in Geneva, it was decided to divide Vietnam into two countries, North and South.

North Vietnam was communist, but there were many people in the South who were supporters of the Communist regime. The Viet-cong (communists from the North) were constantly making forays into the South and receiving help from their supporters in the South. The South Vietnam government which was aligned with the Western powers, was incompetent and unable to handle the attacks from the North. These incursions, too, were in the midst of the Cold War. The U.S. supported South Vietnam, but President Kennedy was far too busy with the unsuccessful venture into Cuba at the Bay of Pigs and the problems developing at the Berlin Wall; so, he never really got seriously involved with matters in Vietnam. In the meantime, the Soviets and China were supplying weapons to the North Vietnamese.

When Lyndon Johnson followed Kennedy after his assassination, he began to add troops to those already in Vietnam until he had a half a million men there. The people in the U.S. were being continually informed that the war was almost won, yet more and more troops were being called for. U.S. citizens were demanding an end to the war and the return of the troops. Anti-war marches were occurring all over the country and there were demonstrations at the Capitol and the Pentagon. Apart from bombing attacks by the U.S. all over North Vietnam, Laos, too, was attacked from the air. In fact, Laos became the most bombed country in the world, considering its size. Nixon followed Johnson who refused to run again for

President because of the opposition he had received from his people as a result of the war in Vietnam. Nixon continued with escalation of the war.

Peace talks finally commenced, but there was no agreement as Ho Chi Minh of North Vietnam demanded total unconditional withdrawal. Finally, in 1973 the U.S. withdrew, and in 1975 Vietnam became united as one nation - a Communist land. Two million Vietnamese were killed in the war, three million were wounded and twelve million became refugees. Almost 60,000 U.S. servicemen were killed, many more were wounded. Post-Traumatic Stress Disorder affected thousands of troops, many of whom had their lives damaged by divorce, inability to settle down, unable to work, and some lives ended in suicide.

WAR IN IRAQ

The war in Iraq commenced in 2003 and concluded in 2011. Why did the United States declare war on Iraq? The reasons given were because Saddam Hussein possessed weapons of mass destruction and was continuing to produce them to use against the U.S. Also, Iraq was supposedly supporting terrorists and was abusing human rights despite the demands of the United Nations. The destruction inflicted upon the World Trade Center on 9/11/2001 was very recent, and America felt vulnerable, especially in the face of Muslim terrorism which had been increasing in the last few years.

The declaration of war was considered illegal by many authorities both within and outside the United States. The invasion was not sanctioned by the United Nations Security Council. Lord Bingham of Britain said that it was vigilantism. Nevertheless, the war plans continued. President George W. Bush and Dick Cheyney, his vice president, spoke on the subject of Iraq possessing weapons of mass destruction on many occasions. Even General Colin Powell, the Secretary for Defense, a well-liked and trustworthy figure repeated at the United Nations Assembly that Iraq possessed and would soon be using weapons of mass destruction against them. Colin Powell's words were accepted as being the truth since he was such a dependable and honest person.

This was a lie. After the invasion no weapons of mass destruction were found. They simply did not exist. Nor was there any true evidence that

Iraq was harboring Osama Bin Laden, the brains behind the World Trade Center bombings of 9/11. We knew that Osama was in Afghanistan, and not in Iraq. The United States, the United Kingdom and Poland invaded Iraq, captured Saddam Hussein and later executed him, and the Baathist government collapsed.

As a result of the war hundreds of thousands of Iraqi soldiers and civilians were killed and there were 3.3 million refugees. Al Qaeda grew in Iraq. They even set up an ISIS (Islamic State) caliphate in the North, which was destroyed at a later date, mainly by the Kurds. With a new Iraq emerging, although in a weakened state, it was doing so as a Shiite state, as the majority of its inhabitants were Shia. Saddam Hussein, who had led Iraq prior to this time had been a Sunni, as was his government. Iran was pleased to have another Shiite state as neighbor, and was available to assist them.

Much blame was placed on the US government for entering the war on a lie without making sure of the details. Very few positive results were achieved in an unnecessary war. There was inadequate war planning and a lack of plans for withdrawal. Poor prison conditions and abuse of prisoners, as well as the high number of casualties and the illegality of the invasion were among some of the complaints. The war also had an adverse effect upon the United States. Terrorism appeared to have increased. The financial cost of the war reached over 6 billion dollars. Damage was done to the respect and reliance that the world had for the U.S. Oil production in Iraq was disrupted and the price of oil and gasoline rose steeply while delivery slowed down, leaving long lines at the pumps. No positive results could be gleaned from the results of this war. There were no benefits for democracy. Perhaps Iran could say that they gained a Shiite government and an ally in the Middle East.

WAR IN AFGHANISTAN

In 1979 Soviet tanks entered Afghanistan in order to stabilize the government there which was Soviet-friendly, but they were not popular with the Afghan people. After much fighting the Soviets were losing their hold to the mujahideen which was anti-Communist. Gorbachev, after coming into power in the USSR, removed the Soviet troops from Afghanistan in

1989 because they were losing too many lives and wasting a great deal of money in the effort. The mujahideen won the battle, but the Taliban, who were Islamist religious conservatives, took over the government.

After 9/11/ 2001 when the World Trade Center and the Pentagon were attacked by Al Qaeda the U.S. asked the Taliban to hand over the Al Qaeda people who were responsible for the attack. It was known that they had been given sanctuary in Afghanistan. When they refused to do so the U.S. invaded Afghanistan while the Taliban, facing defeat, withdrew to the south of the country and into Pakistan. This war actually turned into an international conflict. The U.S. had the opportunity of getting Osama Bin Ladin and many of the Al Qaeda in a cave when fighting in Tora Bora, but they allowed the Afghan troops who were fighting on their side to take the cave while Osama and his followers escaped.

The U.S. went ahead training the Afghans to take over the leadership of their country and their army. They also introduced schooling for the female sex of the country; this had been banned under the Taliban government. Development of institutions was encouraged while Taliban attacks on the civilian population were prevented or countered. The U.S. kept Afghanistan safe from the Taliban.

This went on for twenty years until the U.S. decided to withdraw from Afghanistan. The cost in human lives, together with the billions of dollars in expenses were far too much for the U.S. to sustain. However, the withdrawal was too quick and too sudden that not all the U.S. personnel or Afghan helpers and friends whom they had promised to evacuate, were removed in the little time that was allocated.

The sad story is that the Taliban who had been ruling the country despotically before the U.S. invaded, immediately returned to power as soon as the U.S. withdrew. Women and young girls are now banned from further education. Almost everything that the United States put into Afghanistan has been rejected. Money and human lives, and twenty years have been wasted. Al Qaeda and other forms of terrorism have probably not been affected by a war which does not appear to have achieved anything. The shame is that Afghanistan will be turning back to its dismal past, being led by a very conservative, sexist and narrow-minded Taliban. All the effort put into the country by the U.S., by way of modernization, development of industry and progress in female education appears to have been wasted; money and lives lost. What was gained? Zero. The Taliban were there before the U.S. came, and the Taliban are there now after a 20-year pause.

Of course, we have only discussed what appear to be needless wars that the U.S. have fought in its two hundred-and-fifty years history. There have been necessary wars, such as the War of Independence, World Wars I and II. Few would disagree with the U.S. for going to war against Germany in World War I after the German telegram to Mexico asking Mexico to attack the U.S. or the need to enter into World War II after Pearl Harbor or to rid the world of a crazy, blood-thirsty, racist dictator like Adolph Hitler.

WITHOUT A WHIMPER

*I*f not for Vitamin C South Africa might not have been discovered until much later. When sailors from the Dutch East India Company sailed around the tip of the African continent to India in the sixteenth and seventeenth centuries, they arrived at their destinations with bleeding gums and bruises throughout their bodies. Then they had to get back to Europe along the same route around the Cape, suffering further insults to their bodies. It was decided by the Dutch East India Company authorities to build a garden and grow fruit and vegetables in order to supply Vitamin C to the sailors on their voyages to and from the East. They would stop over at the southern Cape of Africa on their trips in order to get their fresh fruit and vegetables so that Scurvy could be prevented and treated. Thus, the seeds planted in the gardens were also the seeds of a new land where no White man had been before.

Yes, there were Bushmen and Hottentots living there when the Dutch sailors arrived. These are terms that are no longer used. The Hottentots are referred to as the Khoikhoi and the Bushmen are called the San. These are possibly the most ancient people living in the world today; they are closest to the Neanderthals. They are a Stone Age people, with yellow skins which wrinkles early in life. They come from the Kalahari Desert, and have spread all across the southern portion of the African continent. They are hunter-gatherers, and have developed excellent methods for tracking animals and finding plants and roots. During their ventures into plant-life they discovered a root with curare-like effects that they would insert into their arrows for shooting into animals in order to paralyze them, so being more certain of capturing their game. It is estimated that about 200,000 of them were killed in the years following the arrival of the European settlers on South African soil. They have no connection to the Bantu tribes who are from Central Africa and are late arrivals in South Africa long after the Khoi and the San who had already been living there for tens of thousands of years.

After the development of the fruit and vegetable gardens at the Cape a Governor, in the person of Jan van Riebeeck, was sent down to take charge of the newly occupied land. Dutch citizens soon followed in order to live in a place where life would be more quiet and less burdensome, where the climate was better and healthier than in Europe, and where one could live off the land, which was beautiful and so much less crowded. Steadily the population increased. There was no shortage of work-hands. When the Dutch East India Company ships returned from the East they brought back Malays to work the fields and farms, and fruit and vegetable gardens.

Towards the end of the eighteenth century, Napoleon displayed imperial desires in Europe, and there was a fear that he might attempt to send his navy to take over the Cape of Good Hope. The Dutch arranged with the British that the British Navy would be sent to the Cape in order to protect it from any possible designs that Napoleon might have had. However, after the defeat and departure of Napoleon from the European scene, Britain forgot to give the Cape back, thus retaining it as a British colony. Although the Boer settlers would have preferred to have been totally free, they had tolerated control by the Dutch government. However, they were very unhappy to have British leadership. The British did not understand their needs, nor their language. They did not consult with them and treated them like subjects rather than land-developers and partners. To add insult to injury they introduced British settlers from 1820 onwards, especially into the Eastern Cape Province, with whom they displayed a far better relationship.

At the same time the Bantu, coming down from the North, were stealing their cattle and robbing them on their farms. Then the British freed the slaves, which put an end to all the cheap help they had on their farms. There were too many problems - they did not like the British and the discrimination that they had received from them. Now, with the Bantu robbers coming silently at night for their cattle and the products of their farms, it was time to go! They must get away from the British, the Bantu and the new settlers that the British had brought from England!

They packed their wagons, took their belongings and their cattle, and traveled northward and eastward. This was the beginning of the Great Trek of 1836. Suffering unbelievable burdens, traveling by ox wagon over mountains and through rivers, wagons breaking down, wheels falling off, injuries, illness and epidemics affecting them and their horses on a daily basis, and undergoing climate exigencies, yet they moved on. They were attacked by Bantu tribesmen who wanted their possessions, horses and wagons. When the Bantu appeared on the horizon they brought their ox-wagons into a circle (called a lager) and fired at the oncoming warriors through the spokes of the wheels. Thus, they were able to protect themselves.

When they arrived in Natal, they were promised a land deal with Dingaan, the Zulu chief. He invited a group of them into his kraal to finalize the deal. The Zulus fell upon them with knives, murdering as many as they could.

Finally, away from the British in a quiet uninhabited part of the country, they set up two republics, the South African Republic (later called the Transvaal Republic) and the Orange Free State Republic. They established and developed their new lands. However, they still had problems from Bantu raiders. Much of their labors and movable property ended up in the hands of Bantu robbers. Besides, the British whom they had been escaping from, were all around their borders. There was no way in which they could keep them away. Finally, British forces entered Boer territory saying that the Boers had proved themselves to be ungovernable by their own leaders and the British needed to protect them from the Bantu raiders and assist them with their foreign affairs. At first, the Boers seemed to be pleased with the help given by the British because they understood that their problems were becoming too much for them. When all appeared to be quiet and settled, they asked the British to withdraw. Since there was no response to their demands the Boers attacked them repeatedly using guerilla warfare until they finally defeated the British in a battle at Majuba Hill in 1880. This gained for them freedom in their internal affairs, but they were still forced to remain under British suzerainty.

In 1886 gold was discovered on the Witwatersrand, a plateau in the southern part of the South African Republic. This was the largest gold deposit ever discovered in the world. People arrived from distant corners of the globe to participate in, what they expected to be, a free-for-all. The Boers referred to these new residents on their land as Uitlanders (foreigners). The Uitlanders made huge demands to improve their living conditions, and demanded the right to vote. Paul Kruger, the Boer President, would not give in to them for fear of losing power to them. The Uitlanders appealed to the British to help them against the intransigent Afrikaners. Afrikaners were looked upon by the British as a slow-witted, ignorant and simple people. Lord Kitchener said that they were uncivilized, with a white veneer.

Cecil John Rhodes, the great British imperialist who was prime minister of the Cape Province, sent Starr Jameson with forces to the Witwatersrand to stir up the so-called Uitlanders who would join him in the battle, after which he would see that they received the vote and whatever else they wanted. But, to his surprise, they did not join in with Jameson as they had not come to fight (they came for gold). Jameson was forced to retreat in defeat.

Britain amassed forces from the entire Empire along the borders of the two Boer Republics. Paul Kruger demanded that they disband and move away. As they refused to move, the Boers streamed out on horseback, drove them away and laid siege to the cities of Ladysmith, Mafeking and others, which were situated in British South Africa, but outside the Boer Republics. This shocked the British Empire and the entire world. Such a small country of Boers could drive out the forces of Great Britain! It was unheard of! However, the British soon received reinforcements from their Empire, and the Boer War continued for three more years.

The British invented concentration camps, and tens of thousands of Boer women and children were placed there, while thousands died of infections (mostly typhoid). The Boers fought guerilla warfare – no uniforms, no marching, no instruction, no army camps – just a horse and a gun. They remained unseen on a land which they knew very well. They would attack a British depot and disappear into the scenery or into the night or into a home of a friend. Any home would take in a Boer soldier. If the British arrived to search for the person who blew up their stronghold they could not find him. He wore no uniform, carried no gun, the horse was in the stable, or the Boer soldier would have been hidden by the family. They were wonderful horsemen, and they were fighting on their home terrain. The war seemed to be at a stalemate. Nobody was winning, and nobody was losing.

And then after three years the war was over. Nobody expected it to end. The Boers could not understand why. Thet were not losing; they were holding the British at bay. Generals Smuts and Botha and a few other Boer generals foresaw a war that could go on for years with a huge loss in life, so they crossed the British lines and talked to them about a cease-fire. It was time to have peace and to re-build the country. South Africa was granted Dominion status within the British Empire. Many Afrikaners were unhappy that the war was over, but Smuts and Botha convinced the Boers that the war would have gone on for years and the British Empire could never have been defeated. Smuts became a great friend of the British. It was said that he was more British than the British. They made him a Field Marshal. He was on the British War Cabinet in World War II. He was loved by many South Africans, but he was never forgiven by a large percentage of the Afrikaner population for, they said, selling out the country.

When World War I came along many Afrikaners did not want to go to war against Germany because Germany had supplied them with arms to fight Britain during the Boer War. Why should we be on the side of our enemy and fight against our friend? they asked. Nevertheless, many of them played their parts in World Wars I and II. In World War I there was an insurrection by General Maritz, a Boer general, but Smuts quickly put it down. South-West Africa (now Namibia) had been a German colony, but was taken over by South African troops, and after the war the League of Nations gave it to South Africa as a mandated territory.

In World War II many Afrikaners again refused to go to war against Germany. Smuts compromised and promised that there would be no South African forces sent to Europe. They would only fight in Africa to keep Fascism out of the continent. Many leaders of the future Apartheid government spent time in jail during World War II for speaking out against the war. South African troops took over Somaliland, Eritrea and Abyssinia (Ethiopia) from Italy, ending up in North Africa to fight against Rommel.

General Smuts developed numerous enemies amongst his own

Afrikaners. They considered him a traitor, and when the war ended, he, like Churchill, was defeated at the polls. With the defeat of General Smuts, Dr. Malan became the Prime Minister. He was followed by the leaders of the Nationalist Party for the next fifty years. One of the South African leaders following Dr. Malan introduced the policy of apartheid (apartness) which controlled the attitude and laws of South African Whites over the majority Black population.

We were told that Blacks did not wish to live with Whites and Whites did not want to live with Blacks; so, we must live apart - separate, but equal. It was separate, but not equal. Blacks who were not working in essential industries, such as mining, or in private homes were forced to move to the part of the country where they were born or where their ancestors were born. These would be called Homelands, of which there were about eight of them. Industry would be developed there, so they could get jobs in their Homelands. Industry was never brought there, and jobs were scanty. Blacks who were still living in the cities were restricted in where they could stay and where they could eat or seek entertainment. They were not allowed to be roaming in the streets unless they had a 'pass' from their employers stating where they would be and until what time. Most of the people in jail were there because of pass law problems. Separate buses, separate queues for the banks, separate water fountains and park benches were to be available. Black people were not allowed admissions to restaurants, movies and entertainment where White people frequented. They had no vote.

Nelson Mandela arrived on this scene. He was the son of a Xhosa chieftain and educated at Fort Hare, a better class school for higher ranking Black students. He was interested in the political situation. He attended political meetings, spoke a lot and asked questions. He was called a trouble-maker by the Whites. Mandela saw no way out of the morass in which the Black people were living, unless they actively pursued the attainment of civil rights. The White man's paternal benevolence – menial jobs, minimal health care and poor wages - was not enough, he said. Soon, he had to go into hiding because he was wanted by the government because they accused him of attempting to overthrow the government. There was a man-hunt out for him. After months of hiding he was finally captured, arrested, tried and found guilty of treason and trying to overthrow the government.

The sentence was life imprisonment, and he was sent to Robben Island, a prison off the coast of Cape Town.

While in Robben Island he decided, and he directed his fellow prisoners who were found guilty for similar treasonous acts to do the same - not to waste their lives in prison, but to enroll in correspondence courses in law or some other field so that they could get a start to their lives if they should ever be released from jail. When the authorities on Robben Island decided that all Black prisoners must wear short pants Mandela said that they would wear whatever they wished to because the wearing of short pants was meant to place them in an inferior and humiliating position. The order was rescinded.

In the mean-time a referendum amongst the White people in South Africa voted for the establishment of a Republic of South Africa, instead of the previous Union. At the next Commonwealth meeting South Africa was ousted from the British Commonwealth. As a Republic, South Africa thrived. Apart from its apartheid policies it was a country of law and order. It was the most developed country in Africa, producing the most gold and diamonds in the world. It was highly industrialized. It was a bulwark against Communism, and the world knew that Communism would not set foot in Africa as long as the South African government was there. The United States and Britain traded with South Africa and trusted her for its reliability and power. It had a great Air Force and Army. It possessed atomic weapons. South Africa could assure the world that at least one continent would remain communist-free, and other Western lands could leave South Africa to take care of any communist threat in Africa.

No life lives forever. The world was changing. The children of the old Boer farmers studied at the universities and became doctors and lawyers. They did not have to struggle like their forefathers did against climate, the Bantu and the British in order to stay alive. Life was relatively easy for them. The Blacks did not have to be held down; they were already down. Yet the world was beginning to call out "Free Mandela" after he had spent 27 years in prison. People in the U.S. and all over the world were beginning to realize that the Whites of South Africa were living a flourishing life over the 'backs of the Black men'. Countries began to apply sanctions to South Africa and boycotting South African trade. Even sports teams and entertainment artistes omitted South Africa from their world tours. The writing was on the walls.

The government started loosening its bonds on the Black population. Mandela was moved to a prison away from Robben Island, and was treated more humanely in a detention center in Cape Town. He was given his own chef, and taken out for drives. A tailor came to measure him for making suits for him, and he was permitted to receive dignitaries from other lands while still a prisoner. The African National Congress was no longer an illegal organization for the first time in many decades. An election was declared to be held in the near future – an election that was to include, for the first time in history, the non-White population. The President, F.W. de Klerk, called in the International Atomic Commission to dismantle South Africa's nuclear weaponry.

Nelson Mandela ran for President, and won the election. As unbelievable as this story is the Afrikaner leadership withdrew and made room for the new Government that was to be run by the African National Congress, an organization that had been banned. A Black man from a down-trodden people who had never had a vote, a man who was a fugitive from justice and who had been in jail for 27 years was now about to rule the country, including his jailers (the Apartheid government). Without a whimper they just stepped aside – no arguments, no violence, no re-count of the vote and no insurrection. This was like a fairy tale which had come true!

Before the elections it was widely predicted that if Mandela won South Africa would be in for a period of blood-shed and civil war. They said that the Afrikaners would not allow a Black government to rule the country, the Blacks were not capable of running a land with such a large economy (the largest in Africa), an army and air force of top world caliber, and scientific and intellectual advancement of world renown. However, they were all wrong. The transition was co-operative and peaceful. An inhumane brutal regime of apartheid came to an abrupt end. There was no blood-shed, no insurrection. What a change!! The Afrikaners just walked away like good sportsmen who had fairly and squarely lost a rugby match.

This is difficult to believe. It must be a rare case in history where a powerful despotic nation has been overthrown by a weak unarmed class from the lowest caste with no experience in becoming leaders. This is the story of David and Goliath.

Mandela possessed a charisma and inner strength which has been rarely equaled. He was not looking for revenge. He only wished to see equality. He had a sneaking respect for the Afrikaners. He really wanted to see a Rainbow nation working together and surviving side by side. Perhaps he is the only man who could have pulled off such a victory – or as he stated, a victory for both sides.

Since his death, all the original optimism has been waning. The South African government is all Black, but does the ordinary Black citizen have a better life? In some ways the answer is yes. This is the first post-apartheid generation where the Black man has a vote. It was actually given to him (finally) by the apartheid government. He or she is living without increased restrictions as in the past. This was the first generation without segregation and economic restraint. At last, the Black man may walk the streets without a "pass" from his employer to give him permission to be outdoors until a certain time, which he required under the apartheid regime. He may now stand in integrated queues when awaiting service, or drink at the same water fountain as the White people, and he may attend all hotels, movie theaters and restaurants, which he could not do before.

Yet there are persistent problems from the old days that have not altered, and there are many new ones. Inequality still exists. Your kitchen help or your 'house-boy' is still the same person, earning a little more. The poverty is still there, and the percentage of the Black middle class has hardly altered at all. There is very little or no improvement in housing and cost of utilities. Corruption and cronyism have increased, especially by government officials. Theft and graft by community leaders is common. Crime amongst the general population is rampant, including Black on Black. This, together with high unemployment and social inequality disproportionately affecting the Black population makes for a poor economy in the country. The African National Congress promised their people better housing, better health programs, electricity delivered to rural areas. Achievement has been minimal, and the ANC appears to be indifferent. The financial situation of the country is on a downslide. South Africa has one of the worst inequality ratios in the world, according to the United Nations report. It is based on racial lines, not much different than what it was under the apartheid government. The pride of becoming a Rainbow nation is dwindling. There are frequent xenophobic attacks. Many immigrants from other African lands who entered the country following the fall of the White government with the hope inspired by belonging to a Rainbow nation, have been attacked, abused and slaughtered. Murder rates are climbing while other criminal acts appear to be equally out of control.

Many of the Black population have lost faith in the African National Congress whom they say are more interested in their own selves than their people. Some in government have become wealthy while they have very little interest in the futures of the people that they represent. Many of the average Black citizenry have threatened to use their vote against the ANC in forthcoming elections.

Land expropriation from White farmers without paying for the land is a practice that the White farmers do not wish to accept. The Whites are 10% of the population, but they own 70% of the land. Since the Whites grabbed much of the land from the indigenous people many Blacks feel that they should now give it back in order to right the wrongs. There are numerous killings of White farmers, who feel very insecure at home on their farms. They have searched for a safe haven where they could continue with a life of farming which, in many cases, is the only occupation that they know. Hence, there have been migrations of White farmers to Australia, North and South America and elsewhere.

During the apartheid era a prominent Afrikaner stated that God created the Afrikaans people with a unique language, a life philosophy and traditions in order to fulfill a particular destiny in South Africa; we must safeguard all that is peculiar to us and build on it because God has called on us to be servants of his righteousness in this place. This is much like the Manifest Destiny displayed by the American settlers who wished to spread across the entire North American continent, as though it was God's will. Afrikaner identity drew on national, racial and religious belief, and a history of struggle against oppression and natural phenomena. They were in charge and they won. But they are no longer in charge. Where do they stand now? Whiteness has always been important to them, as well as economic progress. Fortunately, they still possess those two characteristics. However, they have to make psychological adjustments since the fall of apartheid. They seem to have distanced themselves from discussing or displaying pride over their past government, and they have withdrawn from the stereotypes of their ancestors who were known to be dour, serious, religious and narrow-minded. They have even forgotten their history and culture of the past, except their language in which they maintain a sense of pride. They remain racists, and admit that they have not come any closer to the Black ruling race since they took over the government. If anything, they have become a little closer to the English-speaking population – basically their enemies in the past, but both White races are losers in the new political set-up. In fact, the Afrikaners also speak more English now than they did in the apartheid days. You might call this situation an alliance among thieves.

Since the defeat of the Apartheid government South Africa has become more Africanized. Less of the European veneer exists. Whereas South Africa was once looked upon as the White southern tip of Africa, it is now a part of Black Africa. As Dr. Verwoerd – the initial developer of apartheid – said many years ago, a little bit of Europe was present in the southern tip of Africa. Africans from the central areas and north are migrating into South Africa, and the country is beginning to look like the rest of the continent. The Afrikaners are pessimistic about the future as they know that a White government will never return. They look upon Apartheid as a golden age gone by. Some Afrikaners who cannot find good jobs feel as though they are being forced out. Hence the migration to pastures new. They are withdrawing, refusing to be a part of the Rainbow Coalition. They fear further Black immigration and genocide, as witnessed in the killing of White farmers and killings in everyday life. They are not even the main Opposition on the parliamentary benches. This 'political animal' of the past seems to have withdrawn from the stage.

The intentions of the post-apartheid government of South Africa were to show the world how a Rainbow Nation would be able to live together harmoniously. Yet counter to these intentions a group of Afrikaners have constructed a town in the dry Karoo in the northern part of the Cape Province close to the Orange River for Afrikaners only. This town was started by members of the family of Dr. Verwoerd, once a Prime Minister of South Africa and the 'architect' of apartheid. He was born in the Netherlands, moved to Southern Rhodesia (known today as Zimbabwe) and later came to South Africa. The town is called Orania. Blacks are not permitted to dwell there or work there. They cannot even buy gas in the environs if they are passing by. It sounds like a 'little apartheid' and totally contrary to Mandela's dreams.

The people living in Orania are only Afrikaners, and claim that it exists for cultural purposes, and not racial. Many are saying that its presence violates the dismantling of segregation, one of the primary actions of the African National Congress. The Afrikaners of Orania say that they will make decisions in their own affairs. Most residents believe that the large cities are all war-zones, and therefore, Orania will keep their inhabitants safe. They think that Afrikaners in other South African cities will be wiped out sooner and more easily than residents of Orania. The population is growing fast, and you can only live there if you promise fidelity to the Afrikaans culture and language. They have developed certain industries there; they sell brick and aluminum to other parts of the country. They have numerous pecan trees, and China buys their pecans.

Legal appeals have been made to the courts for the extermination of Orania, but the courts have done nothing about it. The African National Congress and the government, too, have remained quiet about Orania. They seem to be afraid of causing any disturbances at present, but one cannot predict what will happen in the future. In some hearts 'hope springs eternal', but there seems to be very little chance that this 'mini-apartheid settlement' can survive. Basically, the Afrikaners are no longer the leaders of South Africa, having walked out without a whimper.

WHO ARE YOU?

*I*n days gone by when people had no means for traveling large distances they stayed within a small confined region where they lived, worked, spent their hours of relaxation and died. They were hunters and gatherers. They protected their families from wild people, wild animals and natural phenomena. Those who lived in confined areas looked much alike, as though they had been molded by a cookie-cutter. With the passage of time and the discovery and development of better means of transportation societies began to mix as people moved around from place to place and joined other groups. Today any world-wide traveler can tell you of the different peoples he has come across all over the planet. They are white and black, with colors in between; short and tall, with sizes in between; and fat and thin, and they all talk different languages, while most cannot be understood. They have distinct appearances, and different habits and mannerisms. They pray to different gods and they, like you and I, have fears and loves. We are all different, and yet we are all the same. Who are we?

WHO ARE THE TURKS?

Turkmen came from Central Asia. They had a close relationship to the Mongols, but they do not look like them. They may or may not have had a similar origin. Turkmen were a nomadic people, and wandered southward into Anatolia, which is the main and central portion of Turkey. Turkic people can be found in Turkey, but they are also amongst the Azerbaijanis,

Uzbeks, Kazaks, the Kyrgyz and Uyghurs. All were wandering around South Asia to find a better life in a better place to live. Osman I (1259 to 1326) was the leader of a tribe of Turkmen who fought to make Turkey into an independent state, which later developed into the Ottoman Empire. They borrowed Osman's name. Today Turkey consists of 1/3 European, 1/3 Middle Eastern and 1/3 Turkmen. Religion-wise 85% of the country is Sunni Muslim. This polyglot of Asians and Europeans include Kurds, Armenians, Arabs, Greeks and other south-eastern Europeans. The northern part of Cyprus is also a part of Turkey. The population of Turkey consists of 80 million people. Apart from Muslims there are Christians and Jews living there. The Armenians of Turkey are Christians (who have a national home in Armenia, a neighboring country) while the Kurds are Sunni Muslims, like most of the other Turks.

Before Christianity arrived, Turks were a pagan people. Paul of Tarsus, who went traveling around the Middle East after the death of Jesus, spent much time also preaching in Anatolia and converting many of the pagan people to Christianity. Some of the Epistles from the New Testament are addressed to the people of Anatolia, Ephesus and Cappadocia. After Constantine of the Roman Empire embraced Christianity (until then the Romans were anti-Christian) Christianity became the religion for the entire Empire (fourth century A.D.). Because it was too large, the Roman Empire was later divided into Western and Eastern (or Byzantine) Empires. The Byzantine Empire had its capital in Constantinople, and thereafter Christianity spread further into Turkey. The St. Sophia Church built by Justinian can still be seen in Istanbul. It has since been converted into a mosque by the Islamic invaders who arrived in the 7th century after spreading like wild-fire from the Arabian desert into Turkey, like it had spread into the rest of the Middle East, North Africa and much of the Mediterranean area.

From the time Osman I established a power base in Turkey the Ottoman Empire grew. In 1453 Mehmet II attacked Constantinople, broke through the walls and captured the city, putting an end to the Byzantine Empire, which had outlived its brother, the Roman Empire, by almost a thousand years. Constantinople was on two continents, and, therefore, it was well placed for the Ottoman Empire to advance into Europe and Asia. In Europe, over time, they occupied the Balkans (Greece,

Bulgaria and Serbia) and the Caucasus. Many citizens of these European countries, especially Greeks, came to live in Turkey, thus accounting for the large number of Europeans living there and diluting the Turkmen who originally called Anatolia their home. Middle Easterners, too, came to live in Turkey after the days that most of the Middle East became a part of the Ottoman Empire.

After centuries of occupation, Turkey was no longer able to manage such a large and far-flung Empire. Problems increased and distances were difficult to overcome in a short space of time. Transportation was slow. People all over the Empire began to demand independence. The Ottoman Empire was called the "sick man of Europe" at this time when Turkish influence began to wane. Many countries in the Empire were revolting and asking for independence. The Greeks gained their independence way back in 1830. Other Balkan states also fought for and gained independence later in the century after the First Balkan War. World War I was a disaster for the Ottomans. They had chosen the wrong side – the Germans - as allies. In fact, World War I heralded the end of the Ottoman Empire.

The Young Turks were a growing movement within Turkey at about this time. They played a large part in the development of modern-day Turkey. They entered the scene when the Ottoman Empire's power was waning. They demanded a European-style constitutional government. Kemal Ataturk, the founder of modern Turkey, too, had been a Young Turk. They also demanded religious freedom for other religions, apart from Sunni Islam. Ataturk made sure that there would be a separation between government and religion, with no religious interference from government. The Young Turks Westernized Turkey, separating it from its old Ottoman roots. Apart from suspending religion from government, Ataturk got rid of the fez, brought in Western clothing, Westen alphabet and rid the country of the old Turkish form of writing. In 1923 Ataturk arranged a huge population exchange with Greece. Turkey returned hundreds of thousands of Greeks to Greece and took back similar numbers of Turks from Greece. This way, he saved the lives of numerous Jews from Greece who came to Turkey with the exchange because a decade later Adolph Hitler sent the remaining Jews of Greece to the gas chambers. However, Erdogan, who is the present President of Turkey, is trying to bring Islam back to the Turkish people and into the government, undoing some of the Ataturk reversals.

It is said that the Turks hate the Kurds. Apparently, that is not quite true. They have been living together for many centuries. They are both Sunni Muslims, and in many ways very similar. There are also Kurds living in Iraq and in Syria. The Kurds in all three countries would like to live in a Kurdish country of their own, and be ruled by Kurds. They were overlooked by the Treaty of Versailles and not given any land for a Kurdistan, and are still being rejected whenever they bring up their wish for their own land. So, what Turkey does not like about the Kurds is their desire for a homeland of their own. Turkey does not wish to see her territory disrupted by a breakaway Kurdish nation.

We are also aware of an enmity that has been going on for years between the Turks and the Armenian population in Turkey. During the time of World War I. Turkey was on the side of Germany and the Austro-Hungarians. Turkey was fighting against Russia on the Black Sea in southern Russia. The Armenian homeland was a part of Russia, with a large number of Armenians having spilled into Turkey. The Turks were afraid that the Armenians in Turkey were passing on war information to Russia since both Russians and Armenians were Christians. The Armenian genocide started in 1915, despite the fact that until that time Armenians had been living peacefully in Turkey. Armenians lost their civil rights and were forbidden to bear arms. One million Armenian men, women and children lost their lives in the genocide (statistics differ) which included death marches to Syria. However, this event is denied by Turkey.

Even though there were some Jews from the Middle East living in Turkey from earlier times, their numbers swelled after the Spanish Inquisition in 1492. It is well known that the Sultan of the Ottoman Empire invited the Spanish Jews to come to Turkey in order to escape conversion to Christianity and the loss of their lives. This generous invitation greatly increased the Jewish community in Turkey. The Jews did well by becoming involved in the economy, and remained comfortable and unhindered, especially under Ataturk. Recently, however, President Erdogan, has provoked anti-Israel acts and displayed anti-Semitism. This does not augur well for the future relationship.

WHO ARE THE GREEKS?

The Greeks live in southern Europe between the Ionian Sea to the west and the Aegean Sea to the east, and the Mediterranean Sea to the south. They inhabit the mainland and numerous islands in the vicinity. The Greeks are a mixture of Mediterranean and Alpine people, with a slight Nordic addition. They are probably the same nation as the ancient Greeks, with inclusions from neighboring states through the ages. Their greatest contribution to the world is cultural. They have given to civilization literature, philosophy, architecture, music, medicine, science, knowledge of the human body and sports. Loyalty in Greece rested with the city-state rather than to the country as a whole. Wars were fought between city-states on many occasions; as an example, the Peloponnesian War was between Athens and Sparta.

The Greeks were not outstanding militarily, as it was not their armies that conquered most of the known world, but those of Phillip of Macedonia and after his death, his son, Alexander the Great. Alexander the Great conquered Greece and spread out with succeeding victories as far away as the gates of today's Pakistan and Afghanistan. The Greek culture marched with Alexander and spread to the rest of the conquered territories and beyond. One could say that Greek culture marched on the backs of the Macedonian army. Culture is the most important contribution that Greece has given to civilization – and all this, via a Macedonian, Alexander the Great, and, later, via the Roman Empire.

It was the Romans that defeated the Greeks. Even while the Roman Empire expanded and laid waste to the lands controlled by Greece (between 168 and 30 B.C.), they could not overcome the influence of the Greek culture and the Greek language. Greek was the language of the Roman Empire and the early Christian Church. The first Bible – the Septuagint, was ordered by the Greeks and written in Greek by Jewish scholars in Alexandria (Egypt was a part of the Greek Empire). The works of Homer (the Iliad and the Odyssey) written in the 8th century B.C. arrived wherever Greek influence advanced in Europe. When the Holy Roman Empire ruled over most of Europe the Greek language was still a unifying force.

Greece had a love-hate relationship with Turkey. Ancient Greeks had lived in Anatolia during the Bronze Age, long before Osman and the

Turkmen arrived. They lived in city-states there having come from the Ionian islands. The Roman Empire was split into two sections at the end of the 4th century because it was too large to control. The western portion was called the Byzantine Empire. Only after the Turkmen of Asia started moving into Anatolia did the Byzantine Empire begin to have a problem. The Ottoman Turks finally put an end to the Byzantine Empire in 1453. This was also the end of the original Roman Empire which had lasted since about 250 B.C.

In the 15th century the growing Ottoman Empire conquered Greece. Greeks held high positions in the Empire, both in the army and in government roles. Over the centuries there were continuous rivalries and skirmishes between the two countries until Greece finally received her independence in 1830. There were subsequent wars between Greece and Turkey. Greece seized Salonika, Macedonia and Crete. At this stage the Ottoman Empire was tired, weak and unable to handle its problems, The 'sick man of Europe' was undergoing internal problems and, also finding it difficult to manage such a far-flung mass of territory.

When World War I broke out, Greece remained neutral, but in 1917 she entered the war with the hope of capturing Constantinople – an idea or dream she had had for many centuries because Greece once had control of Anatolia before the days of the Byzantine Empire. When the Ottoman Empire came to an end after World War I Greece invaded Anatolia but was driven back by Ataturk, thus destroying her dreams.

WHO ARE THE RUSSIANS?

About 80% of all Russians are derived from East Slavs, while about 4% are made up of Tartar stock. The old Norse term of Rus refers to men who row. The Norsemen who went westwards are commonly referred to as Vikings, and those who went to the east were the Rus, probably the source of the name of Russia. The Norse were great sailors, living close to the seas and fjords, where they worked on their boats. They were inquisitive and sailed wherever their boats would take them. They sailed down the rivers of Russia, reaching South Russia and the Ukraine, hence the Kievian Rus, which might have been the start of the Russian Empire. There are rivers in Ukraine called Ros and Rusna, coming from the word Rus. The Rus, when exploring the land, often opted not to return home, and settled down when they found an area which looked like the right place to live. They made slaves of the Slavs.

Greeks came to settle around the Black Sea, as did the Goths and Khazars. The Khazars were a Turkic people who had led a nomadic life until they arrived in South Russia. They built homes and converted to a sedentary life. They had no religion, but allowed all religions to be practiced in their domain, which was an invitation to those who had undergone religious persecution to live amongst them. Persecuted Jews, escaping from pogroms, came to live with the Khazars. Many sources have reported that Khazars converted to Judaism, some saying that it was done by large numbers while others have said that the entire nation converted in one swoop. There is very little archeological evidence available, so it is not possible to be sure of the facts.

The Slavs originally were an Indo-European people who came from Persia and northern India, and their language also has Indo-European roots. The bulk of the Russian population is Slavic. Eastern Slavs came to Russia, Belarus and Ukraine. Southern Slavs occupied territory that is today's Serbia. Western Slavs constitute the Czechs and Poles in Eastern Europe. During their travels over Siberia the Slavs traveled peacefully; they did not fight with the local tribesmen as the settlers on the American continent did, decimating the local populations. The Slavs intermarried and assimilated with the native tribespeople. There are Russians who are tall and blonde, who are descended from the Norsemen – the Rus.

In 862 Oleg of Novgorod, a member of the Rus, ruled the Kievian Rus, which existed in the Ukraine. A century later Prince Vladimir converted the Kievian Rus to Christianity. Christianity spread from Ukraine to the rest of Russia. In 1237 the Mongols invaded Russia. They ruled until about 1480 when Ivan the Great freed the Russians from the Mongol hordes.

In 1547 Ivan the Terrible became the first czar of Russia (the word czar is derived from Caesar, as does the German Kaiser). He introduced a reign of terror against the nobility, and also expanded Russia into Siberia. A Romanov became czar at the age of sixteen in 1613. The Romanovs supplied Russia with its czars for the next three hundred years. While Peter the Great (1659 to 1725) was czar of Russia he contributed to the rise of Russia with the building of St. Petersburg, the modernization of the army and navy, the formation of a government, and the introduction of West European culture. He placed Russia on the world map, and made it into a world power with which to be reckoned.

The next important Russian leader was Catherine the Great. She was not Russian, but Austrian who married Peter III. He was like a child, playing with toys and using soldiers to play games with him. Peter III was only czar for about six months when, with the help of Catherine's lover Grigory Orlov, she staged a coup and took over the leadership, announcing that she was Empress. A week later Peter was assassinated. It was never proven that Peter's death was caused by Catherine. She was the longest ruling Russian leader. She encouraged the arts, and brought French influences into Russia. She be-friended and entertained French philosophers of that time, including Voltaire, Rousseau and Diderot. She increased the size of Russian territory and occupied Alaska, bringing Russia on to the American continent.

The Crimean War of 1854 was between Russia and the Ottoman Empire, with Britain and France on the side of the Turks. It was fought by Russia who had demanded protection for the minority Christians and Orthodox Russians at the Holy Places in Palestine which were controlled by the Ottoman Empire. Britain and France looked upon Czar Nicholas I's real intention being a desire of having more influence in the Middle East as a result of a waning and weakening Ottoman Empire. The Czar also misread Britain's plan, thinking that Britain was on his side. Britain and France, however, joined the Turks, and gained their reliance upon them. The Russians were defeated, and crippled by their defeat. The Ottomans gained new trading partners, in Britain and France, after the war. The famous British Charge of the Light Brigade, celebrated in poetry and prose, occurred in this war, as did the work of Florence Nightingale, the British nurse who altered the profession of Nursing forever.

The Communist Revolution came in 1917 after World War II. This put an end to the 300-year rule of the Romanovs (they were assassinated), and the introduction of Communism to Russia. The Bolsheviks under Lenin were now in charge of the Soviet Union. When Stalin was handed the reins of leadership after the death of Lenin, he turned a peasant country into a highly industrialized and military machine. Stalin is responsible for carrying out the Great Purge which commenced in 1934 during which time he put an end to the lives of about 750,000 people – those who were enemies of the Soviet Union, those whom he feared might try to remove his power and others, on suspicion or for little reason. At the beginning of World War II he joined his arch enemy, Adolph Hitler, in invading Poland and sharing the spoils with him, but later he was attacked by Hitler, his ally, and fought a very costly war against him. The Second World War lasted almost six years. The Soviet Union lost a large number of people, suffered millions of casualties, and the countryside suffered severe destruction.

After World War II Winston Churchill warned us about the Iron Curtain which the Soviets were setting up between them and the free world. This was the beginning of the Cold War, the Arms Race (Russians were now producing nuclear bombs) and the Space Race (Russians sent up Sputnik before the U.S. placed a satellite into space). The Cold War lasted about fifty years.

In 1962 the Cuban Missile Crisis brought Khrushchev and President Kennedy into direct confrontation with each other. The Soviet Union was supplying missiles to Cuba who aimed them towards Florida, less than 100 miles away. After much tension between the U.S., Russia and Cuba, the missiles were finally removed from Cuba, and the U.S. in exchange, removed missiles from Turkey that had been aimed at the Soviet Union. Thus, another world conflagration was avoided. There were other such Cold War encounters occurring (described elsewhere).

Mikhal Gorbachev took over the leadership of the Soviet Union in 1985. He introduced glasnost (openness) and perestroika (restructuring of the economy). His intentions were to loosen the authoritarian nature of the Soviet regime. During his period of office, the Chernobyl nuclear disaster occurred near Kiev in Ukraine, causing 150,000 people to become homeless, killing many, and rendering life impossible in that area for 150 years.

Things were beginning to change in the Soviet Union. A general election was held, and Boris Yeltsin won the popular vote. He attempted to introduce a democratic system. In 1991 there was an unsuccessful Communist coup. The failure of the coup caused the Soviet Union to be dissolved. Many of the fifteen Soviet states joined together to form a Confederation of Independent States, but Communism in the old Soviet Union was dead. Yeltsin resigned in 1999, and passed the leadership of

Russia on to Vladimir Putin. Putin was an intelligence officer working for the KGB before he went into politics and worked with Yeltsin until his resignation. He has been accused of having meddled in the US elections in 2016 in order to assist Trump in his presidential bid.

WHO ARE THE PERSIANS?

The Persians are an Indo-European people who speak Farsi, also the name of an area in southern Persia. The name of the country was changed to Iran in 1935 when the Shah of Iran requested all countries to refer to his nation as Iran. It is the name of the country in Farsi, and means the 'land of Aryans'. At the height of its power Persia ruled all the land from Eastern Europe to the Indus River, and included Egypt, Turkey, Afghanistan and India (the part of India which became Pakistan). Cyrus II, the great Persian conqueror, connected the three continents, Europe, Africa and Asia with a system of routes for trade and travel. The Persians initiated the first postal system and, later, commenced a hospital system. Their Empire spread into Turkey, including Cappadocia. Even after the Persian Empire was defeated by Alexander the Great, Cappadocia, despite its separation from the rest of Persia, remained distinctly a Persian town with Persian language and influences.

The original religion of Persia was Zoroastrian, probably the first monotheistic religion in the world. It is a belief of fatalism – life is short and extinction is inevitable so, in the words of Omar Khayyam we need "days of wine and roses". They believe in the world being filled with good and evil, but in the end, there will be victory of good over evil. The religion was founded in the 6th century B.C.E. When Islam arrived in Persia it replaced Zoroastrian. Yet, today it is still practiced by some in Iran, Iraq, Azerbaijan, Uzbekistan, the U.S. and India. The Parsis of India worship through Zoroastrian. It is thought that the monotheistic religions – Judaism, Christianity and Islam – have all been influenced by Zoroaster, the founder.

When Alexander the Great died much of the Empire lost its strength, and Persian rule returned under the Sasanians, who were Persians. Shortly after that, there were two large Empires in the known world, the Byzantine and the Sasanian. Under the Sasanians (225 to 650) the Persian language and culture was revived. The Empire spread and grew because of great military leadership. The Sasanian Empire was there when Islam came to Persia. What is known as Islamic culture in those days was really Sasanian culture taken from the Persians and spread in the Islamic Empire.

When, in the 7th century, Islam arrived in the Sasanian Empire, Persia was taken over by an Arab Caliphate. The Persians were instructed to speak the Arab language, and those who would not or could not were frowned upon and made fun of. The Persians did not like the Arabs. They did not receive high positions in the Caliphate nor were they treated as equals by them. Only after the Abbasid Caliphate moved to Damascus where it became known as the Umayyad Caliphate (661-744) did Persians receive more distinguished roles in the Caliphate.

In 1660 Abbas of Persia, who hated Sunnis, turned Persia into a Shia country. The Persians had always disliked Arabs, and they looked upon them as inferior, uncultured and uneducated. The Shia believe that God appointed Ali, who was Mohammed's cousin, as the Caliph to follow Mohammed after his passing. Instead, Abu Bakr was chosen to do so. Ali, at a later date and following a few Caliphates, was appointed Caliph, but was assassinated during his period of office. He was followed by his son, Hussein, who was trapped in Karbala, Iraq, and then killed – a terrible day which is remembered annually when Shia are clad in black. The Shiites predominate in Iran, Iraq, Bahrain, and are about half the population of Yemen and Lebanon. Beyond that, the rest of the Islamic world is Sunni.

Seven hundred years after the Muslim take-over of Persia the Safavids became the leaders of the country by breaking away from the Ottoman Empire which had now become the center-piece of Islam. The Ottomans, who were Sunni, outlawed Shiism. The Safavids went to war against them and took over control of their own land. They were helped by Ottoman soldiers who had been tortured by their own leaders and fought to escape. Under the Safavids the Persian Empire was stronger than it had ever been. During their domination (15011 to 1736) the Persian culture of old and the language was revived. Silk became a great manufacturing product, for which they were famous. The Empire received its name from the founder. It is said that the Safavids were originally Persian Kurds. They finally fell because they conquered too much territory and were unable to police and protect it. The Ottomans had been their great rivals, and they clashed with them on many occasions – even though the Ottomans, too, were beginning to fail at the same time. Much of the Ottoman culture depended upon what they had learnt from the Safavids.

The Safavids left two major contributions when thy departed. One was Shiism and the Twelver theory which referred to the 12th Caliph who was hidden and never served but is expected to return in the future as a Messiah (Mahdi). The other contribution was the use of gun-powder in war which they used in cannons. The last Shah was a very poor leader, and he allowed the administration to crumble. Afghanistan invaded in 1736, and the Turks and other neighbors started nibbling at pieces of the Empire.

During World War II the Allies overthrew the Shah because it was considered that he was pro-Nazi. He was replaced by a friendly leader. In 1953 the CIA assisted in a coup to overthrow the prime minister of Persia, Mohammad Mossadeq. He had been democratically elected by the people. The coup occurred because Mossadeq nationalized the British-owned Anglo-Persian Oil Company. The coup brought into power the Western-friendly monarch, Reza Pahlevi.

Then came the Iranian Revolution in 1979. The Shah fled, and Khomeini instituted a theocratic republic which was anti-Western. The government was run by clerics. Khomeini threatened to export his Shia theocratic government to other lands in the Middle East. Later that year radical students took 52 hostages at the U.S. embassy in Teheran, hoping to exchange them for the Shah, whom they wanted to punish. The hostages were held for 444 days before they were released, and Khomeini did not get the Shah.

The Iran-Contra Affair was discovered in 1985. The U.S. had been selling weapons to Iran in order to try and facilitate the return of seven hostages taken by Hezbollah. The money coming in from the arms sales was given to the right-wing Contras in Nicaragua in their fight against their regime. President Reagan accepted full responsibility for the Affair.

Iraq and Iran became engaged in a war which started in 1980 and went on for eight years. It was responsible for the deaths of a half million people. Iraq under Saddam Hussein attacked Iran in order to prevent the spread of Shiism by Khomeini and his allies which, they predicted, would interfere with the solidarity of the Baathist Party ruling Iraq. Syria and Libya supported Iran while Saudi Arabia helped to finance Iraq. The U.S.

and the Western world also supported Iraq, only tacitly, because of the dislike for the Khomeini regime. Apparently, nothing really changed as a result of the war; it was a mere waste of life.

Since the 1990s there has been a fear in the Western world that Iran was secretly preparing to develop a nuclear device. If she had the control of such a weapon there would be a huge problem for a large portion of the world. Saudi Arabia and the rest of the Sunni world are afraid that she could enforce Shiism upon them. Israel has been referred to by the Iranian ayatollahs as a terrible country that must be erased off the map. Israel is doing her utmost to stop Iran from developing a nuclear device, working through cyber technology to destroy their nuclear programs. The entire Western world fears a massive conflagration if Iran should develop such a device. President George Bush has referred to Iran as an axis of evil. Sanctions were placed upon Iran to prevent her from continuing in their development of a nuclear device. Sanctions were later eased by an international body in exchange for assurances that nuclear development would cease while Iran would allow regular inspections. President Trump, however, has withdrawn from that Treaty.

WHO ARE THE BRITISH PEOPLE?

The original inhabitants of the British Isles were the Celts who came from Central Europe 2500 years ago. The first Britons were supposed to have had dark skins and blue eyes, but with the lapse of time in a non-tropical climate their skins grew paler, as too much melanin became unnecessary for their colder climate. Today, we know the British to consist of Romans who conquered them when the Roman Empire was expanding in the days before Christ, and Anglo-Saxons, Normans and Vikings when the inquisitive Scandinavians decided to sail from their shores to explore the world in the 8th century. Roman DNA, as well as Scandinavian DNA, can be found in the blood of many people living in the British Isles because of the arrivals and permanent settlement of these foreign Europeans. Before the Romans came to England, the land was known as Albion.

In the 6th century there was a Germanic migration of Anglo-Saxons. After that, everything changed in England. The Roman influence of the past was becoming transformed into a Germanic influence. Whereas the

English language had received many Latin additions, it was now adding Germanic words to it. The Germans were seeking social and political dominance, and were intermarrying with the English. With the 16th century came the religious wars of the Reformation, which again sent many Germans scurrying to England. Some were hoping to go to America from there. George Handel, a German composer, came to England 1n 1712 and spent the rest of his life there, while composing some of his finest music. Many Hessians and other German soldiers fought on the side of Britain during the American Revolution.

George I, Prince of Hanover, was the first German to become King of England. When Queen Anne died, the closest family members were Catholic. A Protestant was required for the position, and George I was the closest, since his mother had died. Therefore, he ascended the British throne, and ever since then many British monarchs married German brides. Until 1917 the British Royal House was known as Saxe-Coburg-Gotha, of German origin. It was changed to the House of Windsor because of anti-German sentiment following World War I. After World War II a large number of British soldiers who had been stationed in Germany, brought home German wives and their children. Many large businesses have been started by German entrepreneurs.

In 1066 William the conqueror and his Norman followers invaded England. The Normans had come from Denmark, Iceland and Norway. They were Northmen (Norsemen) - originally Viking pagan pirates who had ravaged Europe, but finally settled down in France, married and became Christian. In fact, after the Normans conquered England, French was widely spoken in England until the 15th century.

Like the English, the Irish and Scottish people can also trace their line to the Celts. There is Germanic blood in the Scottish people. While some Irish have Spanish blood in their veins resulting from an infusion by sailors from the Spanish armada in the 1500s.

The British monarchy suffered a severe blow in 1649 when a civil war broke out. Many wanted a democracy but Charles I whose autocratic laws had been going against the grain of the British people, refused to compromise. He believed in the Divine Right of Kings, as though he had been appointed by God. The people wanted religious freedom. There was a breakdown between the King and Parliament. His manner of ruling the three Kingdoms of England, Scotland and Ireland was not appreciated.

He was put on trial and executed. Oliver Cromwell, a commoner, took over the reins of government. This period in British history is known as the Interregnum, and lasted until 1660. Charles II, eldest son of Charles I, escaped to Scotland where he tried to get the Scots to help him take back the throne. But the Scots turned him over to the British Parliament. Oliver Cromwell, despite early hopes by the people for of a democratic government, became more autocratic in later years. He distrusted parliament and fought with them. He became more unpopular, and England became more isolated. Europe was afraid that the British disorder might spread to the continent. Cromwell was removed from power, and Charles II was invited to resume the monarchy. Parliament was given more power in a new constitutional monarchy and a Bill of Rights was produced to protect the people.

The British started to develop an Empire at the beginning of the 17th century with the settlement of Jamestown in North America. Other settlements followed in North America, including the Pilgrims in Massachusetts, and there were incursions into Canada. Empire dreams moved towards India, where the Portuguese, Dutch and French rivalled them, but the British took over and ruled all of India from 1854 to 1947. Until the British took over India, India had been governed by local princes and other leaders.

By being loyal to Britain the Indian princes helped the British maintain their rule, and in exchange Britain made it worthwhile for them. By not being a united land, the take-over by Britain was made easy for them. Britain made treaties and alliances with local rajahs, and brought in trade. Clive of the British East India Company ruled with strict military control. He was ambitious and became very wealthy while at the same time he subjugated the rajahs. By an Act of Parliament control was moved from the British East India Company to the Crown. Britain gained financially and was also able to use Indian troops, and less of their own, in order to keep peace in the trouble spots all over the far-flung Empire. Yet Britain finally had to withdraw from India, mostly, the history books will tell you, because of the passive resistance campaign brought on by Mahatma Gandhi.

Others will say it was because of Adolph Hitler. At the end of World War II Britain was in such a poor financial situation that she was not able to maintain and hold on to India. Even if there were no Gandhi and his movement of passive resistance, Britain would have had to give up India. Britain was on the winning side in the war, but on the losing side economically, and in financial straits on account of the war against Hitler.

In the 20th century, the Industrial Revolution spurred the British on in their conquests in Africa and Asia because guns, railways and steamships developed even further. The colonies in the Empire brought them wealth through trade and buying cheap raw materials produced by cheap labor. In exchange Britain brought culture to her colonies, as well as education and democracy. Weakened by World Wars I and II and a change in the world view of colonialism Britain walked out of Empire-building, leaving behind solid well-developed countries which she had developed. At the beginning of the 20th century there were sixteen empires in the world whereas at the end of the 20th century only the United States remained as an empire. Thanks to the British navy Britain became the possessor of the largest Empire that the world had ever known. It stretched over all the continents, except Antarctica. Thus, many British subjects from her vast Empire have been attracted to come and live in the mother country. At the same time numerous Britons have emigrated to the lands which were once members of her Empire – Canada, Australia, New Zealand.

WHO ARE THE HUNGARIANS?

One-half million years ago primitive man lived in Hungary. One hundred thousand years ago Neanderthal man could be found there. Tribes from the Ural Mountains came down in the tenth century, invaded, conquered and migrated to the Carpathian Basin, which is the location of Hungary today. They mixed with Iranian and Turkish people who had already been living there. There, too, was a Mongoloid admixture. The language spoken by these Ural Mountains people was in the Uralic family of languages. It is known as Finno-Ugric. It is similar to the language of Western Siberia in the region of the Urals. It is very strange that no other language in Europe has any similarity to it, except for Finnish and Estonian.

These conquerors from the Urals gave their name to the country. Ugri was the name of the people who came from the Urals. The H might have come from the Huns who were supposed to have invaded earlier – the year 375. The Huns were supposed to have been a cruel and barbaric tribe.

The Vikings who were also invading Europe at the time that the Ugri were conquering Hungary (10th century). They had entered into Russia and the Ukraine. However, they did not go into Hungary as they probably feared the Ugri people.

The Ottoman Empire invaded Hungary in1541. For 150 years Hungary remained in the Ottoman Empire until the Holy Roman Empire sent forces against the Ottomans in the Great Turkish War, whereby most of Hungary was ceded to the Austrian Habsburgs. In 1867 there was a compromise made by the Habsburgs to include Hungary into the Austro-Hungarian Empire. This Empire also included Czechs, Slovakians, Slovenians, Bosnians and Croatians – a confederation of numerous different nations. This Empire lasted until the end of World War I in 1918. Hungarians are considered to be a depressed people – probably a mixture of genetic predisposition and a cultural influence.

After World War I, having been on the losing side, the Austro-Hungarian Empire was forced to break up. Under the influence of Bela Kun, Hungary was led by a Communist government in 1919 which only lasted a few months. The Triple Entente victors of the war set up an economic blockade on the Hungarian Soviet Republic. The Communist government failed and the leaders fled. Bela Kun was executed in the Great Purge in the Soviet Union a few years later.

Between the two world wars the monarchy was restored and Hungary became a bulwark against Communism. During World War II the Hungarians joined up with the Germans. Together with the Axis powers they invaded the USSR. Hungary lost a large number of men in this attack, especially at Stalingrad. When they wished and aimed for a separate peace with the Western Powers they were occupied by the German army. Hungarian Jews were placed in ghettos, and thousands were sent off to Auschwitz. Of 825,000 Jews in Hungary less than one-third survived.

The Soviet war machine invaded Hungary at the end of the war. In 1955 Hungary was forced to join the Warsaw Pact which united all countries in Eastern Europe under Soviet influence. In 1956 there was a spontaneous

Hungarian uprising against the Soviets which was immediately quashed by the Soviet army. Thousands of Hungarians lost their lives, and 250,000 people fled Hungary. Hungary became an independent nation after the fall of the Soviet Union.

WHO ARE THE GERMANS?

The Germans are indigenous to North and Central Europe. They were derived from the ancient Teutons of Northern Europe who were defeated by the spreading Roman Empire in the second century B.C.E. They are Indo-Europeans. They are not Aryans, as Hitler proudly called the German race and looked down upon people who were non-Aryans, like Jews, gypsies and black people.

Aryans are light-skinned Indo-Europeans who settled in Iran and North India, and established the Persian and Indian cultures. They were considered to be superior to the Middle Eastern Semites, to which the Jews had belonged. Hitler's imagination of the interpretation of the word 'Aryan' is without foundation. Hitler's distortions do not make the Germans into Aryans. He considered the word 'Aryan' as being close to the German word 'ehre' which means honor. He saw the Germans as a master race, a nation of supermen capable of dominating the world.

In 800 A.D., after the demise of the Roman Empire, Charlemagne brought his Holy Roman Empire into Germany. Until then there were many German states, cities, areas, all ruled by different governors, leaders or mayors. There was no consistency of a ruling government for all Germany. Germany consisted of separate and numerous tribes. When Otto I was crowned by the Pope as Emperor of the Holy Roman Empire, he was the most powerful ruler since Charlemagne. He became emperor of Saxony and took over the leadership of Germany. Even though the capital of the Holy Roman Empire was not in one place, but moved around, it was usually in different cities of Germany, depending on where the emperor resided or where he wished to have his headquarters. The Holy Roman Empire lasted until Napoleon defeated it at the beginning of the 19th century and made it the Confederation of German States. Not until 1871 did Germany unite as one nation-state in the Prussian-dominated collection of German cities and states.

One of the causes of the Franco-Prussian War of 1870 was a fear in France of the advancing powers of Prussia after she defeated Austria in the war of 1866. France had been aiming for dominance in Europe, and Austrian Habsburgs had been bothering France. However, now Prussia was showing great strength since Otto von Bismarck directed the war to eliminate Austria as a power. When Prince Leopold became a candidate for the throne of Spain France felt as though she would now become hemmed in by an alliance of powerful Prussia and a Prussian-friendly King of Spain. France also feared a unification of the German states (including the southern ones) into one large united Germany, so she declared war on Prussia. The outcome of the War of 1870 was a Prussian victory, with a loss to France at the end of the war of Alsace and Lorraine, which Prussia was delighted to hang on to. The war led to a unification of Germany, resulting in a dominant Germany and a weakened France amongst the European nations.

With a unified Germany and a French desire for the return of Alsace and Lorraine the stage was set for World War I. Revanchism was the term for revenge that France sought for the loss of Alsace-Lorraine. While Europe sensed that all the tension was working up to a war in Europe the Archduke Franz Ferdinand of the Austro-Hungarian Empire was assassinated in Sarajevo. This sudden eruption warmed up the scene for World War I, and was the casus belli for the conflagration.

Europe became divided into the Central Powers which included Germany, the Austro-Hungarian Empire and the Ottoman Empire while the Allies consisted of Britain (and her Empire), France and Russia. After four years of war, Germany lost about two to three million men and 13% of its land, much of which produced iron and coal. Alsace and Lorraine went back to France. Germany was in huge debt and the people were humiliated. The navy mutinied and the army was unable to provide further support. The reparations demanded by the Allies were very large.

The Treaty of Versailles made huge demands upon Germany, apart from inflicting guilt upon the country. The debt imposed upon Germany was impossible to pay when the country was in such a poor economic condition. How ccould Germany pay the debt if she was bankrupt? There was unrest and disillusionment. The kaiser fled to Holland and the Weimar Republic was set up as the new government. Nothing could be done by the government in the face of hyper-inflation, poverty, lack of food and clothing. There was rioting and there were little revolutions, and even an attempted Communist coup. The Treaty of Versailles left no room for Germany to re-build and start a new life. The Treaty of Versailles made it possible for Adolph Hitler to enter on to the scene like a Messiah and promise a new world for Germany. The Treaty of Versailles was also the most important cause of World War II.

Hitler was elected as the Fuhrer by popular vote. He promised to rescue Germany from the devastation and unfair Treaty of Versailles. The people had been so psychologically wounded, depressed and suffering physically from the great loss which they had endured that they were prepared to grab on to any word of hope. How did Hitler re-build the country which was in such devastation, physically and psychologically? He borrowed money and started reversing the financial status of the country. He disregarded the debts imposed by the Treaty of Versailles. He started re-constructing the military and naval forces despite the prohibitions set down by Versailles, which disallowed re-armament. European countries were tired of war, and did little to re-arm themselves or even think about it. The League of Nations did nothing to stop Hitler. His immediate hatred was for the Jews, and his goal was to rid Europe, if not the world, of them. He occupied Sudetenland, a portion of Czechoslovakia where there was a large German population, and then he occupied the rest of Czechoslovakia, followed by Austria where he was welcomed. Nobody lifted a hand to stop him. Even though Hitler hated Communism he made a Non-Aggression Pact with the Soviets. Yet before 1939 was over Hitler and the Soviets marched into Poland, which was the commencement of World War II – and the beginning of the end for him.

Wars had changed since World War I. Instead of fighting from trenches, this new war was fought mainly in the air and at sea, mainly with U-boats (and submarines). World War II spread further than the relatively confined World War I. It was fought in Europe, in the Mediterranean, in North Africa, in Asia and in the Pacific. Thanks to the Japanese attack on Pearl Harbor, America, who had hitherto remained neutral, came into the war. Without American help, Hitler could well have won the second world war. After six years of death and destruction the Germans were defeated.

The Holocaust was a state-sponsored murder of European Jews by

Hitler. The word comes from the Greek 'burnt offering'. He was responsible for the demise of 2/3 of the European Jewish population. At the Wannsee Conference in Germany Hitler's Final Solution for the Jews was presented to Nazi leaders and members of the German government. He kept his word, and the Jews of Europe were taken to Belsen and Auschwitz and numerous other camps where they were shot or gassed.

At the end of the war Germany was divided into four occupational zones – Soviet, American, British and French. Berlin, which was well within the Soviet zone, was similarly divided. This occupation by the Allies lasted for ten years. The Soviets had total control of East Germany. The return to full economic power in Germany in such a short time was a miracle. It was helped by the Marshall Plan and the supply by the United States of heavy machinery and other equipment. The U.S. gave Germany 23 billion dollars. Added to all that, was hard work put into re-building of the nation by the German population. German manufactured goods were of high quality and in great demand.

There are about 80 million Germans living in Germany today. Apart from Germans living in Austria and all over the world. The brutality of the Nazi regime from 1933 to the end of World War II is well-known. All those with liberal views were suppressed, exiled or placed in camps. Jews and gypsies were slaughtered, labor unions disallowed and most religions made to feel unwelcome. Despotic rule was present, and the masses submitted to it. In fact, Hitler was elected by the people. He was so popular because he said that he would defy the Versailles Treaty and make Germany great again. He was like a Messiah who had come to save his people.

WHO ARE THE IBERIANS?

The Iberian Peninsula lies in the south-western corner of Europe. In some ways it appears to be isolated from the rest of Europe by the Pyrenees. The Phoenicians had been sailing to the south-western peninsula of Europe ever since Biblical days, and had settled there. The ancient Greeks did much exploring of the peninsula while it was a Roman colony. The Romans occupied this territory in 217 B.C.E. and held on to it for six hundred years. The Iberian Peninsula supplied the Romans with silver, olive oil, food and metals. The Vandals and Visigoths drove out the Romans when the Empire started to fail and could no longer hold them back.

In the 7th century the Muslims conquered the Peninsula. Iberia was not one or two countries, but consisted of numerous little kingdoms. It was conquered by the Muslims through the Umayyad Caliphate, employing Arabs and North African Berbers, referred to as Moors. They drove out the Visigoths who had ruled the Peninsula for two centuries, and the Umayyads called the land Al Andalus. Islam spread by conquest, and then they introduced trade and the work of missionaries. This was the Golden Age of the Muslims in Spain, when culture and architecture developed.

After many years the northern part of the Iberian Peninsula was gradually taken over by the Christians who ruled in Aragon and Castille, and to the west was the Kingdom of Portugal, which had also taken over the islands of the Azores and Madeira. The Christians began a steady penetration in a southerly direction in an attempt to gain control over Muslim territory. This process was known as Reconquista, which was encouraged by their growing pride of being Christian and a feeling of national identity. The process of Reconquista lasted 780 years, having commenced in 711. Why did it take so long? Because not only were the Christians fighting against the Muslims, but they were also fighting among themselves.

When the Moors originally arrived in Toledo, the Jews who had suffered severe discrimination from the Christian authorities assisted them in their occupation of Toledo, which was the capital of Castille. Jews seemed to have flourished very well living under the Moors. However, when in 1085 Reconquista occurred in Toledo and the Christians returned to the control of the city, they came back with a vengeance upon the Jews. The Jews faced conversions, mass killings and blood baths. There was rioting again in Toledo in 1118 as a result of discriminatory laws inflicted upon them by Christians. Subsequently, multiple other periods of persecution followed.

The Christians finally drove the Moors out of Spain in 1492, and followed up their victory with the Spanish Inquisition – re-enacted by Portugal some years later – whereby all Jews were to convert to Catholicism or else face exile or death. The status of exile of Jews from Spain lasted five hundred years, ending towards the end of the 20th century.

Coinciding with the Spanish Inquisition was the commencement of the exploration of the world by Spain and Portugal. Remember that Prince Henry the Navigator of Portugal had sent out ships down the west coast of Africa in the first half of the 15th century (Prince Henry died in 1460), where they discovered land which Europe had not known of its existence until then. However, these ships were not able to safely sail into the high seas because of the lack of information as to where they were. Prince Henry's ships were forced to hug the coast-line.

Abraham Zacuto, an astronomer and Rabbi, living in Spain before and during the Inquisition, advanced the workings of the ancient astrolabe by adding astronomic tables and maritime charts which enabled ships to sail deep into the ocean and know where they were. This new astrolabe helped Christopher Columbus to arrive in the New World and allowed Magellan to circum-navigate the world. Zacuto was exiled from Spain as a result of the Inquisition, He then went to Portugal where he became the King's astronomer. When the Portuguese Inquisition came, he was exiled again! These exiles certainly showed a lack of appreciation for a man who enabled Columbus and Magellan to make their discoveries!

What influenced these countries to send men sailing into these unknown seas and discover new lands? Europe had known about the wonderful spices from the East that would enhance the taste of their food and keep it from rotting so quickly. This, and the possibility of finding gold and other valuable metals were incentives to search and find. Also, there was the desire to spread Christianity to the natives who could not possibly have heard about it.

So, they set out to sea and made remarkable discoveries of new lands that nobody had ever heard of. They sent in armed forces, subdued the natives and built forts to protect themselves. Spain and Portugal became countries with the largest and most powerful empires in the world at that time. Spain consolidated her holdings in the Caribbean, South America and the south-western portion of North America. Portugal was more interested in Africa (Angola and Mozambique) and Asia (India), although they also developed their interests in Brazil. They brought back spices, gold and heavy metals; and where they found no gold, they developed crops. They exchanged plants and goods with the natives, and helped spread Christianity. While bargaining for gold and crops they inadvertently gave the natives the diseases of Europe, like smallpox and measles, against which the natives had little or no immunity.

After the Jews and Arabs were driven out of Spain, the population of the country decreased and the output of the land diminished, while the plague became rife. The economy suffered and a Depression ensued. However, the Spanish Empire was beginning to grow as a result of the conquistadors, and Spain put a lot of energy in developing her Empire. Gold was coming into the country from the South American colonies while Christianity was spreading in the Americas because of the hard work put into proselytization by Spain. Because of its Empire Spain was becoming the most powerful country in Europe.

During the 16th and 17th centuries Spain was ruled by Habsburg kings, who came from the renowned family of Habsburgs who ruled the Austro-Hungarian Empire. Royal marriages in Europe at that time helped to consolidate alliances and strengthen Empires. When Isabella of Spain died her daughter Joanna succeeded her. She married Philip, son of Maximillian I, a Habsburg. Soon after that Joanna became insane and Philip took over as Regent. Thus, the Habsburgs entered the Spanish throne. Spain contracted alliances with European powers and was a world power for some time. The last Spanish Habsburg died in 1700, and there was no official heir to the throne. There was a choice of choosing one from France or Austria, but Britain would not allow an heir from France, her enemy. In 1713 the Treaty of Utrecht, following a war between France and Britain fought in Europe and America, removed the Netherlands and territories in Italy from Spanish control. Thereafter a weakened Spain struggled along. Spanish colonies, hankering for independence, fought against Mother Spain, and gradually each, in turn, gained their freedom.

In 1898 the Spanish-American war was fought. The U.S. supported the Cuban desire for independence while she also wished to protect her business interests in and with Cuba. At the same time the U.S.S. Maine was sunk in Havana Harbor. At this pretext the U.S. went to war with Spain, assuming that the ship was sunk by Spain. The cause of the loss of the Maine was actually a fire on the ship, unrelated to any Spanish interference. The war further weakened Spain when Cuba, Guam, Puerto Rico and the Philippines changed hands and became American possessions.

The Spanish Civil War lasted from 1936 to 1939, and it was due to a failure of democracy – a refusal to compromise. It was fought between the left-wing Democrats, called the Republicans, and the right-wing army rebels and upper classes, referred to as the Nationalists. Francisco Franco led the Nationalists, and he was assisted by other Fascists, in the persons of Adolph Hitler and Benito Mussolini, and also by the Catholic Church. The Nationalists won, the monarchy was abolished and a republic was set up under Franco who ruled until his death in 1975.

Franco kept Spain out of World War II even though Nazi Germany and Fascist Italy had helped him in his Civil War. He was bound to the United States because they were giving him financial aid in order to recover his country after the civil war, and he did not want to lose that help. Also, he was afraid to enter in the war because Britain could easily invade the Canary Islands and Morocco, within easy grasp of the Royal Navy in the Mediterranean.

WHO ARE THE FRENCH?

Julius Caesar conquered Gaul in 58 B.C.E., and Gaul remained a Roman province until the Western section of the Roman Empire came to an end. During the 4th century Gaul turned towards Christianity which had become the religion of the Empire. During the 5th century A.D., a Germanic people conquered Gaul, the land that is known today as France. They were the Franks who gave their name to the country. In 732 the Umayyad Muslims, after conquering Spain, moved into France in an attempt at conquest, but were driven back by Charles Martel.

In 768 Charlemagne became King of the Franks. He united the Franks who had been existing as separate tribes living in France, the Netherlands and Belgium. Charlemagne founded the Holy Roman Empire, and was crowned as the Holy Roman Emperor by the Pope in 800. The new Holy Roman Empire took on the name of ancient Rome, even though its stronghold was moved to Germany. It was felt that the words 'holy' and 'Rome' would be great assets in the name. Charlemagne united Western Europe for the first time since the Romans and helped spread Christianity through Europe. He allowed local cultures and laws to remain throughout his domain. After he died in 814 the HRE was weakened.

Viking raids into France occurred from 820 to about 920. They came for gold and silver, and also for wives and slaves. Apparently, there was a shortage of females, because the higher classes in Scandinavia grabbed up most of the women. Women became a sought-after commodity. The Vikings besieged Paris on more than one occasion. Normandy was raided by the Vikings, called the Norsemen or North men in France – hence the name of Normandy, whence came William the Conqueror in 1066. Many of them settled in Normandy.

After Charlemagne, France was ruled by kings until the French Revolution at the end of the 18th century when the Revolution removed the monarchy and introduced a republican form of government. Napoleon Bonaparte grabbed control of the country, soon making himself Emperor. Within a few years most of Europe fell into his hands. His accomplishments included the Napoleonic Code, whereby he introduced freedom of religion, eliminated privileges for those born amongst the wealthy, reorganized military training and warfare, and made contributions towards education. He was finally defeated by the British, under the Duke of Wellington, and a coalition of European countries at Waterloo in Belgium in 1814.

The defeat of Napoleon brought on the restoration of the Bourbons – the reigning monarchy before the French Revolution. The brother of the last King – Louis XVI – succeeded Napoleon. The Bourbons continued to reign until 1830 when Charles X was ousted because of his introduction of restrictive ordinances which were contrary to the spirit of the 1814 charter, which had been compiled after Napoleon was defeated. Charles was followed by Louis-Philippe, a cousin of the outgoing monarch.

In 1848 Louis-Philippe was overthrown because of unemployment, food shortages, riots and general economic collapse. This introduced the Second Republic. It also aggravated the general European discontent that was spreading and leading to revolutions in Germany (still not united), Italy, Austria, Denmark, Belgium and Ukraine. These revolts were mostly against monarchies, but the majority of them failed and caused disillusionment amongst the people.

Louis Napoleon, the nephew of Napoleon Bonaparte was elected as President. He soon had himself crowned as Napoleon III. His goal was to expand the French Empire. He got himself involved in a number of wars. He entered into the Crimean War in 1853 against Russia, where he proved to be successful Then he fought against Austria in 1859; this war was followed by an economic recession. In 1870 he took on Prussia – a big mistake – as he lost the war and had to give up Alsace and Lorraine. The monarchy was abolished for the third time in seventy years.

At this stage the Industrial Revolution was in full swing in Europe. In France industry was expanding and construction of railway lines was spreading. A period known as Belle Epoque was heralded into France. Progressive socialist movements developed. Art and culture became widespread, and many people from all over the world came to live in France so as to be in the vanguard of the developing culture. The turbulent first half of the nineteenth century had given way to peaceful living and cultural development.

The French had a hatred for Germans, mainly because they had taken Alsace and Lorraine from them in the Franco-Prussian War of 1870. They began to sidle up to Russia and Britain since they realized that they needed friends. The desire to build an Empire like the British had done was still uppermost in their minds.

However, in 1914 France was forced into World War I because she had a treaty with Russia that either side would help the other if war broke out. The Austro-Hungarian Empire had declared was on Serbia when the Archduke Ferdinand was killed by a Serb in Sarajevo. Germany immediately joined with Austro-Hungary and attacked Russia. The main focus of the war was moved to France, where most of the rest of the war was fought. French eyes were set upon Alsace-Lorraine, and France saw an opportunity to get it back. The Treaty of Versailles which ended the war was also a major cause of World War II because it was very harsh upon Germany, not allowing Germany to recover or pull itself together. When World War II arrived with the invasion of Poland by Hitler's Germany and the Soviet Union, France was forced to join in on account of previous treaties.

Germany made short shrift of France in World War II, defeating them in a few weeks in 1940. The southern portion of France, the overseas empire and the naval forces were left in the hands of the Vichy government, an approved pro-German leadership under ex-war hero Marshal Petain. Germany was too busy fighting World War II to have any time to deal with minor matters, such as taking care of the French colonies. At the end of the war the Allies marched into Paris led by General de Gaulle, the Free French leader.

After World War II, France would have been in very difficult straits, but they, like many other European countries, were rescued by the American Marshall Plan. This helped to stimulate many French industries.

WHO ARE THE ITALIANS?

Are the Italians the same people as the ancient Romans? For the most part, yes. They are a Romance ethnic group. There are additions from neighboring European lands, and also people from the Italian empire in Africa prior to World War II, who came to live in Italy. There has also been a diaspora from Italy to other lands. There are about 15 million people with Italian ancestry living in the United States, mostly from southern Italy. Many Italians have migrated to South America.

Rome was founded in 753 B.C. with the help of Romulus and Remus, if you believe it. The Romans were originally of Indo-European descent. Apart from the Roman portion of the Italian peninsula there was also an Etruscan region. Before the Roman Empire developed, Rome was ruled by Etruscan kings. Once the Roman Empire existed, it gathered up all the city-sates into its fold into one country, which remained united until Rome fell. The Roman Republic also spread into and absorbed Sicily, Corsica and Sardinia. The Roman Empire then advanced throughout most of Europe, including Gaul and Britain. It also conquered much of the Middle East and North Africa. When it became too large it split up into the western Roman Empire and the Byzantine Empire. In the 4th century Constantine brought Christianity to the Roman Empire. Prior to that Christians were not popular in Roman domains.

In the 3rd century, the Roman Empire almost collapsed because of civil war, strife and anarchy. Diocletian restored stability, but, nevertheless, Rome continued to decline. The western Roman Empire was attacked by the Goths in 410 A.D., which heralded its demise. They had been grappling with the problem of barbarian races attacking their borders for many years; first the Goths, a Germanic tribe, and then the Vandals. After Rome fell it was governed by a Germanic emperor.

When Charlemagne was anointed emperor of Rome in 800, Rome

became a part of the Holy Roman Empire. There was no country called Italy after Rome fell, until 1871. It existed until then as a number of different countries fighting their own wars or belonging to other lands until Cavour united Italy under one King, Victor Emanuel II.

Before the unification of Italy, it consisted of a number of smaller countries – Piedmont, Savoy, Lombardy, Venice Genoa, the Papal states and Sicily. Sicilians were a little different from the other Italians. They were mostly of mixed heritage. Adding to their Italian background, they received genes from surrounding lands due to their Mediterranean location, including Arab, Byzantine and Jewish stock. This can be noticed in their appearance and from their language.

Commencing in the 1860s and culminating in 1871, Italy became unified. Cavour (through diplomacy and forging an alliance with France against Austria) and Garibaldi (who fought to win over Rome, the last obstacle), managed to forge Italy into one country. Popes never accepted the new Italy until 1929.

After World War I Italy went on a colony-seeking mission of Africa gaining Libya, Eritrea, Abyssinia and Somaliland. Between the two world wars Benito Mussolini took over the government of Italy, and introduced Fascism to its people. When Adolph Hitler became the Fuhrer of Germany Mussolini found an ally. Mussolini fought on the side of Germany in World War II, but the Italian forces did very little to assist Germany. Italy lost all her colonies, and towards the end of the war Italy was occupied by the Allies. Mussolini was hung in the streets by his own people.

Some have asked why did Italy not receive any punishment from the Allies at the end of World War II, as was the case with Germany and Japan. It is true that Germany was occupied by four Allied Powers and was divided by a wall (as was Berlin too) and Japan lost its Empire and its army. The reason that Italy suffered far less, was because it was occupied and defeated by the Allies. After Mussolini was killed and Fascism came to an end, Italy joined the Allies in 1943 and fought against their previous partner, Germany. Post-war Fascism was purged by the Italian people, and Italy became a republic. They did not require any assistance from the Allies.

WHO ARE THE JAPANESE?

There are about 129 million people of Japanese descent. The word comes from the 'sun's origin'. They originated in north-east Asia, and are of Mongoloid descent. They settled in the islands of the archipelago known today as Japan. The original Japanese were called Ainu. There are a few different religions in Japan – Shintoism (a polytheistic religion), Buddhism (a religion without a god), Confucianism (focusing on ethics, morality and ancestral worship) and very little Christianity (banned until 1873). The Shinto religion, for which Japan is most famous, has no book like the Bible or Koran. Unlike Western religions where one practices a particular religion, in Japan one is permitted to have a combination of religions. You could be a Shinto for some things and practice Buddhism for others.

Why are there so many words in Japanese that resemble Hebrew? 'Shamas' in Hebrew means a guard or warrior, while in Japanese, Samurai means the same. 'Hagar' in Hebrew and 'Hakaru' in Japanese means to investigate. In Hebrew 'malchuto' means kingdom, whereas in Japanese the word is 'mikoto'. Again, in Hebrew 'Horeb' means perish while in Japanese 'horebu' means perish. 'Ata' in Hebrew and 'anta' in Japanese means you. A priest in Herew is 'kohane' while a priest in Japanese is 'koyone'. Hebrew 'teura' and Japanese "teru means to shine. In Hebrew there is an expression 'hadak hashem', which means tread down the name; the same expression in Japanese is 'hazuk ashime'. The list goes on endlessly.

Yet the two countries are thousands of miles apart, and there is no mention in history that the two peoples ever got together. If your memory can go back to 570 B.C.E., you will remember that Israel was attacked and defeated by the Assyrians, and the Jews were exiled from their land. These jews were considered to exist no longer, and they are referred to as the Ten Lost Tribes. Since then, it has been realized that the tribes probably were not lost, but there have been settlements of Jews in India (Karala and Bombay), China (Kaufeng), the Lemba of South Africa, Ethiopia; These are probably the wandering Jews of the Ten Lost tribes. So why could they not have gone to Japan, especially as they were as far away as China?

There are also many holidays in Japan which are identical to what has been described in the Hebrew Bible, such as when God asked Abraham to sacrifice his first-born to him (and later changed his mind), when King

David moved the Ark to Jerusalem. These are all celebrated and acted out annually in Japan, even though the Japanese don't read or follow the Hebrew Bible. By the way, the Emperor's palace is built according to the measurements of the Temple and guarded by two lions, as in Jerusalem, even though there have never been lions in Japan. Are you surprised to hear that during the Second World War, after Hitler invaded Lithuania he called for the authorities to send him all the Jews so they could be placed in his concentration camps. The Japanese ambassador for that part of Europe tried to get visas to Japan for as many Jews as he could, but as the visas were not forth-coming he started printing as many visas as he could, saving thousands of Jews from the death camps. Don't forget that Germany and Japan were Allies in the war. Is it not strange that this happened? After the war this ambassador died, and many Jews whose lives he had saved went to his funeral in Japan.

One other interesting situation involving Japan and the Jews. There were many Jews who escaped from Europe during the war, who were living in Shanghai. Japan, Hitler's partner in the war, had invaded China and was in control of Shanghai, but they did not harm or do anything to upset the Jews. By the time that Mao took over China, the Jews left.

The first Europeans to arrive in Japan were Portuguese sailors who were exploring the East for spices, gold and other precious metals. They introduced Catholicism, guns and gun-powder. It was the guns that altered the style of fighting for the Japanese warrior class, the samurai. Before the Samurai, Japan was ruled by aristocrats and others born to higher classes. The Samurai took over and ruled from 1185 until 1876. In 1635 the Shogunate decreed that there will not be any foreign influence in Japan. Christianity, too, was banned because it taught the worship of one God, which the Shogunate feared because that would threaten their authority.

This decree lasted over 200 years until Commander Perry of the United States arrived on a ship in Tokyo harbor in 1853 demanding to speak to representatives of the Emperor. When he did not receive what he came for he came back the following year with the same request. This time he was able to make a treaty which opened the doors of Japan to trade and to protect the rights of Americans. Thereafter Japan started modernizing her country and copying what she learnt from the West. The Meiji Restoration occurred in 1876, after the Samurai rule ended. The feudal system was abolished, a new learning system for schools was introduced. Government was brought into the country with a cabinet system. Isolation came to an end following Perry's visit. This occurred at the same time as Japan was becoming urbanized.

Apparently, President Theodore Roosevelt had something to do with the rise of Japan. When he visited Asia, his opinion was that the Chinese were a nation going downhill while the Japanese were smart, quick to learn and had a great future. The Japanese should be able to lead the Asian people with American assistance. He told the Japanese authorities what he thought, and encouraged them in this pursuit. He congratulated them on their attainment of Korea when they attacked them. He never thought that one day they would become so powerful and even go to war with the United States, as they did after bombing Pearl Harbor.

In 1904 the Russian port of Vladivostok was iced in and the weather conditions did not allow the port to be used for shipping. The Russians were seeking a port to the south to enable them to continue their export trade. They sought a port in Korea, which was under Japanese control. Russia thought that the northern portion of Korea should be neutral. Japan attacked Russia for her expansionist policy, and defeated her leaving Russia weakened – this was prior to World War I.

During World War I Japan was very helpful by bringing her ships into the Mediterranean, assisted with moving supplies and troops for the Western allies. They were even rewarded with a number of Pacific islands which were handed over to them for their services. In 1931, fresh from a number of victories, Japan invaded Manchuria and occupied it. In 1937 they invaded China. Their excuses were that they needed space for their growing population, but, more likely, they were looking for fuel, steel and other resources for their growing industrialization.

The Japanese joined the Axis partners, Hitler and Mussolini in World War II. They invaded and took over Malaya, Singapore, French Indo-China, the Philippines and numerous Pacific Islands. They bombed Pearl Harbor in Hawaii on 'that day of infamy' (according to FDR). This was like a suicidal event because it created Japan's demise as far as her war-like ambitions were concerned. The Pearl Harbor attack brought America into World War II, which not only helped to defeat Japan, but also got rid of Adolph Hitler, Nazism and Fascism. It took two nuclear bombs, one on

Hiroshima and one on Nagasaki, killing about 120 thousand people before Japan finally surrendered.

After the war their economy was devastated, but with the help of the United States they grew back rapidly. They showed skill in the work force, and concentrated on their recovery. Their industries began to thrive, as did their growth in technology. They were permitted to keep their emperor, provided he did not interfere in governing. The government was democratic and displayed stability. They also demonstrated peaceful co-existence with other nations. The U.S. promised them military protection, if required. They co-operated with General Douglas MacArthur, who directed their country on behalf of the Allies.

WHO ARE THE CHINESE PEOPLE?

The history of Chinese civilization goes back about 6,000 years, making it the oldest nation on earth. It is also the possessor of the oldest written language, but it has no alphabet because the writing is done in pictographs. It is a large country, only a little smaller than the United States, but it has only one time-zone, probably because of convenience. The Han Chinese constitute the majority of the population of China (over 90%). 18% of the population of the world are Chinese.

The ancient Chinese invented paper, the compass, gunpowder and printing. They were the first to use kites. The Chinese were able to produce silk before anyone else learnt how to make use of the silk-worm. Round about two hundred years before the birth of Christ they understood the action of the heart and the human circulation. William Harvey was the first person in the Western world who described the circulation in the human body in the 17th century A.D. – almost two thousand years after the Chinese.

During the long history of China there have been about thirteen dynasties, each contributing in trade, culture, morality, philosophy and religion to the common welfare. Yet all was not always peaceful, as there were many local wars. The origin of the Chinese people was not in China, but in Africa – East Africa, and from there they found their way to Asia. Anthropologically, Peking Man was supposed to have lived in north China a half a million years ago, but the Chinese people of today are not the descendants of Peking Man – scientists believe that they are more likely to have come from Africa.

Marco Polo was the first European to have visited China, which he called Cathay. The name China probably comes from the first Qin dynasty which started the rule by emperors. Imperial rule only ended in 1912, the last of whom were the Manchu emperors. They were overthrown by Sun Yat Sen. China had become frustrated with the everlasting run of emperors while a growing feeling of nationalism was entering the minds of the people. Sun Yat Sen led the revolution and paved the way for re-unification of China. He died shortly after. Chiang Kai Shek soon led the Chinese people, but the Communist Party started stirring, and before long Chiang realized that there was more than one problem ahead. There was the Japanese invasion of China, but there was also a threat from inside, which was Mao Tse Tung and his Communist Party.

Mao wanted to destroy capitalism in China and also traditional elements from the past. He wished to introduce Marxism. He fought a civil war against Chiang, finally, but not until the United States had defeated Japan in World War II. Mao and the Communists drove Chiang out of mainland China. They sought refuge in Taiwan, an island off China. Chiang set up his government there while Mao declared the creation of the Peoples Republic of China in 1949. He rid the nation of warlords, and proceeded to improve the lot of women by increasing their educational standards. At the same time, he had a falling-out with his friend, the Soviet Union as a result of doctrinal differences. Marxism tends to be more theoretical as compared to Communism. It is also slower in its development and accomplishments, whereas Communism was prepared to rush to war in order to achieve its goals.

The Great Leap Forward (1958 to 1960) occurred during the time that Mao was trying to establish collectivization and nationalization of the economy together with a common ownership of production. There would be no class distinction. He was trying to improve food and industrial production. Unfortunately, the Grear Leap Forward resulted in a terrible famine killing 30 million people – the greatest death incidence from famine in history. It failed because China was not sufficiently prepared to handle such a huge nation under the Marxist-Leninist system; there was insufficient know-how.

Subsequent to Mao, Deng Xiaoping became Chairman. He succeeded in opening China to the world, and improved Chinese international trade. In 1989 there was a major protest at Tiananmen Square in Beijing which was led by students. The government responded by bringing out troops and tanks, while many rioters were massacred. Access to information was controlled, journalists attempting to send out reports were jailed and foreign journalists were expelled. Thus, no reliable statistics are available. No fair trials were held.

At present Xi Jinping is the leader of China. He has been there since 2013, and it has been decided that he may remain as president as long as he wishes to. China is still considered to be a Communist country, but with certain divergences from Marxist-Leninism. Since the 1980s China has altered from a planned socialist economy to a mixed economy, which almost resembles a capitalist economy. The Chinese authorities claim that their economy is guided by Party control while they maintain a socialist course for the people.

"Veni, Vidi, Vici" cried out Julius Caesar. "I came, I saw, I conquered". That is half the story of the history of mankind. But it goes on from there. Man did not rest. He could also have said "I learnt, I taught, I built". Civilized man excelled in art, literature, construction of cities and skyscrapers, of healing the sick and travelling to the stars. He was able to show that he was worthy of his ability in developing the world into a better place to live for himself and for those who would follow him on this earth. However, through greed and hatred, jealousy and fear, Man is also destroying what he has created. He has developed means of killing with weapons of war that will put an end to his enemies and his friends, as well as his mother and brother. We seem to have out-smarted ourselves. In this book, we have completed our Journey into Yesterday. I wonder if, one day, our offspring will be here to make a Voyage into Tomorrow!

Printed in the United States
by Baker & Taylor Publisher Services